Praise for Pano

'The literary find of the year'
—Annie Proulx

'Karnezis's writing has intensity and directness,
as he takes on the relationships between humans
and their gods.'
—Kate Saunders, *The Times*

'Unexpectedly haunting, its details catching like
splinters in that part of the imagination that
responds to pure storytelling.'
—*Times Literary Supplement*

'Gripping and worldly-wise ... a novelist
who is already well-respected but deserves
to be better known.'
—Phil Baker, *Sunday Times*

'A master storyteller.'
—*The Independent*

'Worthy of Graham Greene ... an outlandish,
ingeniously constructed novel as powerful and
full of surprises as any ancient myth.'
—*Sunday Telegraph*

'A novelist of unusual gifts.'
—*Financial Times*

we
are
made
of earth

PANOS
KARNEZIS

First published in 2019 by
Myriad Editions
www.myriadeditions.com

Myriad Editions
An imprint of New Internationalist Publications
The Old Music Hall, 106–108 Cowley Rd, Oxford OX4 1JE

First printing
1 3 5 7 9 10 8 6 4 2

A CIP catalogue record for this book
is available from the British Library

ISBN (pbk): 978-1-912408-27-6
ISBN (ebk): 978-1-912408-28-3

Designed and typeset in Palatino
by WatchWord Editorial Services, London

Printed and bound in Great Britain
by Clays Ltd, Elcograf S.p.A.

For Olivia

One

THEY KNEW THEY were lost because they had been travelling for several hours but still had not arrived. When the sun's disc broke above the sea, they saw nothing to raise their hopes, no sign of an island in any direction. At midday, still with no land in sight, someone said that the man who sold them the boat had fooled them. The men began to curse, the women raised their hands in prayer and the children cried, until the teacher silenced them all with a calm voice, saying that he had seen a map in the town the day before and it was just as the smuggler had said: their destination was less than ten nautical miles from the beach from which they had set off. So then they turned to the man at the tiller and swore at him, grabbed him by the collar, slapped him, shook him with a force that rocked the crowded boat dangerously until the teacher announced, again in his unperturbed manner, which made everyone stop and listen to him, that even though in all likelihood they had missed their destination they could still use the sun and a watch to navigate their way back to the shore which, the previous night, they thought they had left behind for ever.

His words were greeted with sighs of relief and praises to God, who had put the sun in the sky. A different man took his place at the outboard motor, opened the throttle and turned the boat around. The sun was out but it was cold and windy and the sea, which had been rough during the night, was turning rougher. There were those who already suffered from seasickness but there was nothing else to worry about because the man who had taken it upon himself to save them reassured them that at the speed they were travelling they ought, according to his calculations, to reach their destination in less than two hours.

Mokdad sat quietly near the front of the rubber dinghy, quivering with the cold—or was it with fear? He was dressed lightly for that late autumn day and there were no warmer clothes in his backpack either. He had misjudged the ferocity of the Mediterranean, just as he had underestimated the difficulty of his whole month-long journey to the coast. Most of the people aboard had come across each other for the first time on the beach the previous night, but everyone already knew that one was a teacher, another the mayor of a small town, a third a gentlemen's tailor and Mokdad a doctor, a piece of information they had received without comment but with a lingering look of disapproval which had made him avert his eyes.

The prow of the large inflatable dinghy splashed through the waves and for a while everyone was happy again apart from the tailor, a small man wrapped in an oversized orange life-jacket, who was vomiting over the side. In their brief time together on the beach the previous night, he had confided to Mokdad that he could not swim. Out of the two families with children on board, one did not include the father: a woman, twin girls, and a boy with closely cropped hair. The boy's unruliness attracted the baleful glares of the teacher, who stood with one foot on the prow, like a sea captain from the Age of Discovery, setting the course with his compass. Mokdad had not spoken to him so far in the journey but had listened to him speak to someone else in beautiful Levantine Arabic, his voice bowing under the weight of an erudition that one did not normally associate with a primary school teacher. And indeed, in the course of that conversation the man had revealed that he was also a bit of a local historian, a pastime that gave him greater pleasure than the teaching of children, whom he had not been shy of saying he did not like much.

They travelled for a few minutes before the outboard motor sputtered and fell silent. All eyes turned to the man at the tiller with the suspicion that he was to blame, and watched while he pulled the starter rope again and again, but the motor would not start and he picked up the fuel tank and shook it: it was empty. There were cries, more despairing than angry this time, and the faith in God of everyone but the most pious was shaken to its foundation, a hopelessness that eased a little when the teacher produced a pair of plastic oars. The men took turns at them, but it was difficult to row in the rough sea and they made very slow progress. At dusk they could still see no land, and the teacher told them to stop for the day because without the sun he could not tell which direction they ought to be travelling.

As soon as the sun disappeared the temperature dropped quickly, and the evening became colder than their previous night at sea. Swaths of brown, red and orange marked the horizon, and a yellowish glow where the sun had been a moment earlier, but higher up the bright colours faded to grey and clouds were gathering. The waves were big but slow-moving, with crests that did not break, lifting the boat quite high and taking it down again in a gentle movement. Soon no one was talking, even those praying turned silent, and the only sounds were the splash of the waves and someone sobbing. The wind skimming the waves sent clouds of spray into the boat, but there was nowhere to take shelter and gradually everyone got soaking wet. As night fell the wind built up, the waves grew bigger and stronger and the boat was thrown about with force. There was a narrow crescent moon out, not bright enough to light the surface of the water but it gave the sky a dark shade of blue-grey, which marked it out from the inky blackness of the sea. A voice in the dark demanded water but there was no reply. The voice repeated the question with impatience but no one answered this time either, and Mokdad could just about see the tailor, bloated by his life-jacket, harassing those around him until someone gave him a shove and told him to leave them alone.

Mokdad shivered in wet clothes, sitting wedged between two other passengers to whom he had not spoken during the journey. Unable to resist his tiredness, he eventually fell asleep without wanting to, and when he opened his eyes again he saw that he was sitting in water. Everyone was shouting and trying to stand, holding up their luggage. They were starting to rock the boat and the teacher shouted at them to sit down but they did not listen. The waves kept tossing the dinghy about, causing the standing passengers to lose their balance, and they grabbed each other to steady themselves, but still they would not sit in the flooded hull.

A few passengers were trying to empty the water with their hands, and the teacher was still trying to pull down those standing, when another wave struck, the boat tipped and everyone fell overboard. The water was freezing and the weight of his clothes made it very hard for Mokdad to stay above the surface. Quickly he took off his jacket and shoes and looked for his rucksack in the dark. It was beyond his reach already and he tried to swim towards it, but he was surrounded by other passengers and their suitcases and bags, many of which had scattered their contents on the surface of the water. All his money was in the rucksack; he tried to find a way through the flapping arms and the floating luggage but the waves held him back. There was an opening in the crowd and he made an attempt to swim towards it, but a hand grabbed him and he turned to see the tailor struggling, even in his oversized life-jacket. Mokdad abandoned his effort to get to his rucksack and stayed with him.

Those closer to the upturned dinghy tried to climb on it, but there was nothing to grab hold of on its rubber tubes and they kept slipping back into the water. Everyone was screaming and the waves crashed against the dinghy, which lurched this and that way, hitting those near it; those who could not swim well went underwater. Among the people the doctor saw the twin daughters of the woman without a husband, holding hands as they, too, tried to stay above the surface. He could not see their mother or little brother anywhere. When they stretched an arm at him, saying something he could not hear in the noise of the storm, he made to swim towards them, but the tailor's hand again stopped him.

Mokdad turned and shouted at him, 'Let me go!'

The tailor held him by the collar. 'No, no. Don't leave me, please.'

'Take your hands away! They're drowning! Let me go!'

'Don't leave me alone,' the man whimpered.

'Let me go, damn you!' Mokdad tried to free himself but the man tightened his grip.

'Let me go, you fool!' Mokdad shouted.

'Stay with me. I can't swim. I… I… I…'

'Get your hands off me!'

But still the man did not let go and they struggled for a while before Mokdad freed himself. As he finally pulled away and turned his head, he saw the two girls go under the waves. They did not come up to the surface again.

In a rush of anger he grabbed the tailor by his life-jacket. The man yelped and tried to fight him off this time like a child, which made the doctor even angrier and he began to pull the life-jacket off him. He was not thinking; all he could see was the plastic orange jacket, and he felt a blind urge to take it away from the man who could not swim. The loose jacket came off over his head easily, while the small man was trying to stay on the surface and fight the doctor off at the same time. Mokdad tossed it into the waves, too far for the man to get it back, and only then, his anger satisfied, did he come to his senses. The tailor, his arms flailing, was swallowing water, and the doctor shouted at him to calm down and move his legs and arms. He seemed to be doing it, but when the waves brought Mokdad closer to him the man grabbed hold of him with both hands and they went under together.

The doctor kicked and moved his arms to come back to the surface. His mouth broke out of the water and he took several deep breaths before trying to haul the other man up, too. The tailor offered very little help, but with great effort Mokdad managed to get him back to the surface. The man spat water and coughed and breathed rapidly, still holding Mokdad tightly around the waist, a dead weight on the doctor, who was struggling to keep both of them afloat. The effort was exhausting, he had trouble breathing and his strength was ebbing away but he could not give up, thinking of what he had done. He looked around for anything to help the two of them float and saw a suitcase, which he could just about touch if he stretched out his hand. But, even though he tried many times, he was unable to grab it. Then the tailor began to sink again and this time Mokdad had no strength to pull him up. And the man would still not let him go: they went underwater again. This time the doctor panicked and tried to prise the hands off him, but the other held him very tightly as they sank deeper and deeper. He could not see him—he could see nothing, it was completely dark.

He began to push and scratch the other man, his movements slowed by the water; he hit him in the stomach, poked his eyes with his fingers until finally, when he could no longer hold his breath, he escaped from him and swam to the surface, where he gulped air, shaking with horror. He looked around in the near dark but there was no one near enough to have witnessed what had happened. He saw his rucksack not too far away this time but he barely had any strength; he could do little more than keep afloat. He stayed where he was, watching his rucksack with all his money bobbing up and down on the waves until it disappeared. He thought about the man he had killed.

The wind skimmed over the waves and spray struck his face, making it difficult to see what was going on around him. Squinting, he thought he could see others in the water among scattered pieces of luggage. He wanted to stay within sight of them but did not attempt to get closer, afraid that there might be more who could not swim. Again he wondered whether anyone else had seen what he had done. Suddenly something gave him a hard blow on the back of his head, and he turned to see the rubber prow of the dinghy, which the waves had carried in his direction. He dived to avoid being hit again and when he came up there was a long rope trailing from the boat in front of him. He grabbed it. The wind and the waves continued to toss the boat and Mokdad was dragged along, feeling safer as he held on to the unsinkable dinghy via the rope. Now that he was no longer struggling to survive, he began to feel the coldness of the water again, in his feet and hands, which had gone numb, and his head hurt from the blow he had received from the boat.

The orange life-jacket was floating away. Someone grabbed it: it was the twins' little brother, who was beating his hands to stay above the water. The dinghy was blown towards him, too, and within a moment Mokdad reached him and got hold of him. The boy was not heavy but it was still hard to swim with the extra weight. He let go of him again and tried to climb on to the upturned dinghy, but he could not; nor did he manage to push the boy on it. Holding the rope with one hand, with his other he helped the boy put on the life-jacket, then tied the rope around both the boy's and his own wrists; he let the boat drag them away from the others. He could hear them for some time afterwards, then the noise of the storm covered their screams and Mokdad and the boy were alone.

With the moon now blocked by the clouds, the sky was just as dark as the sea and there was no horizon. All this time the boy had said nothing; he was just staring at the doctor. Mokdad said, over the wind and the splashing of the waves, 'Hold on to the life-jacket. It'll keep you afloat.'

The boy said, 'The life-jacket. I saw you.'

Now that there was a witness after all, Mokdad's secret became a crime. He wondered what the boy thought about it. He had not sounded threatening or appalled—more like fascinated. Perhaps in his young mind there was such thing as righteous killing and death made perfect sense; his thoughts were not yet tainted by doubt and despair.

Mokdad said, 'Rest a little. Then we'll try to climb on the boat again.'

The wind was still blowing hard, and the dinghy dragged them along on its blind voyage into the night. In the next lull in the storm Mokdad swam up to the boat, untied the rope from the boy's wrist, took up the slack and held on to it with both hands against the dinghy to stop himself from going under while the boy climbed on his shoulders. The boy's weight still forced him underwater, but he held his breath until the child had crawled on to the upturned plastic hull. When his turn came, with no one to help him, he could not climb up, but then he had the idea to swim to the stern and pull himself up from the outboard motor.

At last he was out of the water. Even though he was still cold, the numbness in his feet and hands began to recede. He took the rope that had saved them, which was tied to the bow eye of the dinghy, stretched it, and tied its other end to the motor, so that it ran along the length of the hull and the boy and he had something to hold on to when the waves tossed the boat about. He sat down with his legs on either side of the boy and wrapped his arms around his small body to keep him warm while holding on to the rope, too.

'Have a rest. What's your name?'

'Jamil.'

'I won't let go, Jamil. I promise.'

Warmed by the man and the life-jacket, the boy fell asleep. The large dinghy was more stable capsized than right side up and there was no danger of its tipping over despite the rough sea. Mokdad watched out for the other passengers in the dark, but the boat had travelled far from them already and he could not see or hear anyone. There were only pieces of luggage, open suitcases and clothes and shoes scattered over the water bobbing up and down. All night he tried to stay awake but would drift off, only for a jolt of the boat to wake him up. It would take him a few seconds to understand where he was, then he would make another effort to stay awake, but within minutes his bleary eyes would shut again and he would quickly fall into deep sleep.

At daybreak the sky was roofed with dense bluish storm clouds, which moved together, and a narrow horizon glowed with the grey light of dawn. The debris of the previous night was gone and there was no sign of what had happened. Lightning flashed: Mokdad judged that it was very far away because he neither heard thunder nor saw rain, but the sea was still rough and he held the sleeping boy in his arms while grabbing the rope with both hands until the wind eased and the sea settled into a tall but slow swell. There were a few gaps in the distant clouds where shafts of sunlight slanted through. He could see quite far but the horizon was as empty as the day before, an emptiness that struck him with fear. The sea felt like a wall built around the rubber boat without a way out. He shut his eyes and waited for the pounding of his heart to ease, telling himself that as long as they stayed on the dinghy they would be found. He shivered in his wet clothes, which the cold air would not dry; his hair was matted with salt and he wondered how long they would survive without water. But he could forget his fear briefly if he thought about the previous night. He tried to reassure himself that the tailor might still be alive, that at the last moment, while sinking, somehow the man had had the strength to kick his legs and move his arms and swim back up to the surface. But, even if that had happened, the man could not swim, and the boy was wearing his life-jacket now.

By midday the sky had cleared and the sea was almost calm. The boat bobbed up and down with a much lighter swell, giving the impression that it was hardly moving. Mokdad had had nothing to eat since the evening of their departure, but it was his thirst that was making him suffer, and he made it worse by washing his face with sea water and then unthinkingly licking his lips. Later something brushed against the dinghy. He saw it out of the corner of his eye and at first thought that he had imagined it, but when he looked in the water he saw a few inches below

the surface a school of enormous brown jellyfish travelling
blindly past the dinghy.

Jamil woke up and asked for water. He was sullen
when he was told that there was none, and asked if he
could drink from the sea.

'No, it would make you sick,' Mokdad said.

The boy made a grimace of annoyance. 'What are we
going to do?'

'We have to wait,' Mokdad said. 'They'll come for us.'

'When?'

'I don't know. Soon.'

But Mokdad did not quite believe it. A group of
strangers on a clandestine crossing…who would raise the
alarm?

Jamil moved to the stern and played with the
outboard motor, turning it this way and that, betraying
not the slightest hint of grief for the death of his mother
and sisters. Perhaps he believed that the women had
survived and he would soon be reunited with them. But
Mokdad doubted that. There was something about the
child's manner—his nonchalance, his absence of any
emotion other than annoyance and evident boredom, his
inexpressive face—that struck him as all the more callous
because of his youth.

The storm had passed and there was no danger of
falling off the boat. But it was still cold. For the rest of the
day they said little to each other. The following morning
the doctor was the first to open his eyes again, woken
by his need for water. It was torture now; his mouth felt
very dry, and moving his tongue about produced almost

no saliva. He stared at the horizon, no longer wishing for a warm day, which would make his thirst worse.

The swell slowly turned the boat around. It had gone almost full circle when he thought that he saw, at a great distance, the vague outline of land. He stared at it for a long time, unable to decide whether he truly saw it or it was some kind of mirage until the sun rose higher, the day grew warmer and out of the blue haze emerged the smooth and unmistakable shape of an island. He shook the boy awake and pointed it out to him.

'Look, look,' Mokdad said. 'Do you see it?'

'Where…?' Jamil replied drowsily.

'There. Don't you see it? Land. Can you see?'

'Yes…yes.'

'An island,' Mokdad said. 'Look.'

'How far is it?'

For a long time the sea pushed them towards it, but then the current changed direction. Mokdad made the decision to abandon the dinghy, even though they were still far from the island, and try to swim towards it. Several hours later they came ashore on a beach strewn with flotsam. Jamil took off the life-jacket and they sat on the pebbles facing the sea and trembling from exhaustion and the cold breeze. The ground swayed under them. Mokdad only had to close his eyes to feel that he was still perched on the capsized dinghy, but he was on firm ground, alive and cold and exhausted and desperately thirsty, the salty taste still on his cracked lips. What did his survival mean? That he was forgiven for his crime? Perhaps saving the boy's life had been his atonement and he could stop feeling guilty about what he had done; but the presence of the child, who knew what had happened, reminded him of it. He wished that he were alone.

A small bell chimed somewhere and they both turned at once and looked, startled, in the direction of the pines farther back from the beach. From among the trees an Asian elephant was shyly looking at them.

Two

IT WAS NOT OFTEN that the inhabitants of the island, one of those small pieces of land that remain perpetually hidden under a dog-eared corner of the map, had the opportunity to entertain themselves, even though Damianos, dressed in a white hat and summer suit, would never accuse them of being particularly hard to please. There were the daily consolations of television, whose weak signal was relayed by a station on a much larger island many hundreds of miles away, and the annual visit, every spring, of a one-man shadow theatre, which gave a few performances for the children in the town square after dusk, a show that generated more laughs among the grown-ups than the younger members of the audience. For the rest of the time the people were easy prey for anything unusual that sparked their curiosity and would talk about it for days afterwards, no matter how trivial. A new arrival, a departure, an accident, the weather of course, a birth or a death even those that were wholly anticipated: anything could set off a myriad discussions, many of them starting in the only coffee shop in town, from which they quickly spread, with the story changing, intentionally or not, with each retelling, so that when it made its way back to the patrons of the shop a few days later it was often so unrecognisable that it gained a new lease of life and could do the rounds of the town again.

They talked about his wife and him of course. He had not heard them, not with his own ears, but he could tell from the way they stared at him in the street or the coffee shop where he only went to escape a blustery wind—and on the quay that morning where despite the cold wind quite a few men, women and children had gathered at the ancient tramp freighter swaying at her moorings to watch the loading of his old Bengal tiger.

In his orange and brown striped coat, which he wore like a royal cloak, Rajanya was a splendid specimen whatever his age. The small rusty cage that contained him, the fate of so many royals throughout history, did nothing to subdue his pride, the stare of his amber eyes, or the roars with which he bade the crowd a not-so-fond farewell.

For more than six months on the island the cat, too, had been the source of many stories shared among the locals: he had belonged to a maharaja; he had killed a British ambassador and had to be smuggled out of India; the natives (whom the islanders imagined in Ottoman slippers, billowing trousers and turbans) had sacrificed virgins to him; he was now being sold to a billionaire from an Arctic country to be turned into a coat or a hearthrug. Only the rumour that he was leaving turned out to be true, and there he was now, his cage tied to the crane of the ship whose bearded captain in khaki uniform and peaked cap stood on the quay. He inspected the chains, gave the all-clear and the cat was slowly winched off the ground in silence: it was as if the crowd were witnessing a magical levitation. Halfway up, the crane gave a jerk, and the cage swung and banged loudly against the hull. The spectators let out a groan of disapproval, someone on deck cursed, the boom of the crane moved farther out from the ship and the tiger resumed his ascent with greater caution. The operation was completed without further incident.

Watching at some distance from the crowd, Damianos's face contorted in a grimace of pain, and to his embarrassment and against all his efforts a few tears trickled down his cheeks. He wiped them away as carefully as if they were evidence of a crime. When he put his handkerchief away, his forehead creased into his habitual frown. The captain, who had a reputation for coarseness but could burst into tears at the first notes of the most hackneyed love song, saw him even though he had been standing some distance away. He approached with a wide smile and asked him whether he was all right.

'It's the wind, captain,' Damianos said. 'It makes one's eyes water.'

The captain pushed back his cap and agreed in a commiserative voice, even though, he said, he much preferred the cold winds and rough seas of winter to the heat of the summer months. 'It'll be winter soon,' he said. 'It's quite cold already, no? It can get pretty cold on these islands.' And added, 'Rest assured, Mr Damianos, we'll take good care of him.'

'Don't let anyone get too close. He'll snatch your arm before you know it.'

'I understand.'

'Did you get the meat?'

The captain nodded dutifully. Damianos had given him enough to feed the animal for two weeks, which would normally be more than enough time to reach the mainland, but the sudden storms at that time of the year and the old engines of the ship, which often broke down, did not quite allow the man to say so with full confidence. Perhaps he should have given him more food, Damianos thought. But it was too late for that now. He did not say anything.

When the cage was lowered into the hold the crowd began to disperse. Only Damianos stayed where he was, frowning at the old freighter and shivering under his summer clothes. Someone who knew him well could tell that his stare, despite his frown, was despondent rather than critical, but the captain, who had only met him a few days before, interpreted it the wrong way and hurried to reassure him. 'She's a good ship. In rude health, as it were. All she needs is a fresh coat of paint.'

There was no reaction from the other man and he tried again, a little indignant, to draw his attention away from the sorry sight of the ship at the quay. 'Did you hear about it? We came across a shipwreck.'

Damianos looked at him for the first time that morning. 'A shipwreck?'

'Floating suitcases. Clothes scattered all round. We didn't see anyone. I don't know what they were doing so far south. I guess they were lost.'

'Did you search for them?'

'Search? We aren't the coastguard, Mr Damianos. I radioed it in.'

'That's terrible,' Damianos said, and took his eyes away from the captain.

It was a troubling answer because of its ambiguity, intended or not, and left the captain wondering whether the man was dismayed at the human tragedy or at his, the captain's, apparent callousness. He was about to say that the law of the sea nowhere stated that he had to search for the owners of floating suitcases, but then thought more calmly that to argue about legalistic principles risked making him sound even more hard-hearted. He opted for the wisdom of silence. A moment later an overloaded three-wheeled cargo motorcycle arrived and the captain mumbled an excuse and went to oversee the loading of its freight on to his ship.

Damianos reverted to his earlier contemplation but the cold was making him more and more uncomfortable: his hands were shaking, his nose was running, yet he still refused to walk away from the quay. Rajanya had gone very cheaply, he knew that, even considering the cat's age. He had fetched about half of what Damianos had paid for him five years ago, but there had been very few offers when he'd put him up for sale and he was desperate for money.

Only if one had stood close to him for a while, and waited patiently, would one have begun, after Damianos had wiped his nose for the third time, to guess some of his thoughts. He was not gazing at the sea now but at the small group of children who had stayed behind after the crowd of onlookers left the quay. The captain beckoned them over and Damianos could hear him promising them a tour of the ship if they helped him unload the motorcycle. One girl, no older than ten, tall for her age, thin, dressed in shorts and flip-flops, reminded Damianos of his daughter. Anna, Anna: her name blasted out his other thoughts and the memory of her face flickered for a moment. He tried to fix it in his mind's eye but it began to dissolve almost immediately, fading like a ghost. Stay, he thought, stay a little longer… But she was gone. Rajanya's muffled roar came from the hold of the ship and, as if suddenly realising that there was no longer any reason to be there, Damianos went away.

His wife had asked him to do something in town but he could not remember what. Oh, it would come to him eventually… At the shipping agency he took a deep breath and walked in. The blinds were lowered; the desk was buried under loose sheets of paper and heavy ledgers, everything covered in dust. The pedestal fan that had run all summer had been replaced by a paraffin heater whose bad odour he gladly forgave in return for its warmth. The walls were decorated with framed photographs of freighters, ferries and cruisers steaming into a future that judging by the faded colours had long become the distant past. He paused and looked at them with his hands clasped behind his back, feigning airiness, using the opportunity to delay the serious discussion he had come to have, despite his eagerness to speak to the man at the desk.

'That one is in a cove down from where you're camped,' the agent said, seeing him studying one of the photographs.

'What? The ship?'

'Yes. It ran aground in the eighties. Bad storm, old ship... They left it there. Not a good place to swim. A woman drowned there a few years back. She was the head teacher at the school here. She taught my son.'

'How terrible.'

It was the second time that Damianos had used that word that day, but it would be wrong to assume that he had done so frivolously on either occasion. He never used it flippantly even though he had been using it several times a day recently, repeated to himself in his mind like a mantra until he fell asleep at night.

'A spinster,' the other man said with a glint in his eye. 'She'd failed the boy in Classics twice.'

Damianos winced. Under different circumstances, in happier times, he might have come up with a witty rejoinder himself, but he no longer found comments like that

22

amusing. He sat down in the only other chair in the office and put his hat on the desk with a discreet movement that nevertheless drew the agent's attention; the man smiled again. 'That is a nice hat,' he said.

His visitor looked at it as if he were seeing it for the first time. The white Panama hat next to the yellowed sheets of paper and the dusty ledgers struck him as an aptly arranged still life on the theme of futility: the only thing missing was a skull. It was an unpleasant image and he sought to drive it out of his mind with a reply that, similar to a reflex response, escaped his mouth before the words had the chance to confer with his mind. 'You like it? You can have it,' he said. 'It's not new but in excellent condition. I don't care for it any more.'

Reluctantly, and perhaps suspiciously, the man took the hat, inspected it inside and out, then tried it on. There was no mirror in the office to confirm that the hat suited him, but its size felt right and his visitor was nodding appreciatively, so he accepted it with thanks and hung it on the stand in the corner of the room, far from the reach of its former owner, who might be tempted to change his mind and take it back. Then the shipping agent sat back at the desk without any expression of gratitude.

It was a bad sign. Damianos finally asked him the question he had come for.

'I've come to enquire about the loan. I hope you've had time to think about it. How about it?'

'I can't,' the man said without hesitation.

'I see,' Damianos said. He clenched his fists under the desk but his expression did not change. 'As I said, it's only a matter of a few months. I am prepared to sign any paper you like. You'll be the first to get paid as soon as I can afford it.'

'I'm afraid it's impossible.'

The shipping agent glanced at the hat on the stand, fearing perhaps that the gift would be revoked, but his visitor, already on his feet, did not think of it until he came out of the warm office and began to shudder again with the cold. His head, whose receded hairline left it defenceless against the blustery winds, suffered more than any other part of his body. He regretted offering the man his hat. He loved that hat. How foolish it had been to let the man have it. A policy of appeasement did not work. It hadn't worked with Hitler either. Nazi, Damianos thought, angry with himself.

The fishing boats were tied to the jetties, the loading of the ship had been completed, and the children and motorcycle were gone. Dark smoke was rising from the ship's funnel and through an open porthole her engines growled. A row of bay trees and iron benches lined the esplanade. Damianos imagined an ambitious mayor envious of popular seaside resorts, hoping to create a little Côte d'Azur in this unsung corner of the Mediterranean. Only the trees had thrived; the ornate benches had rotted away. He left the waterfront to avoid the wind and through a narrow street came to the flagged square with the white church at one end. When he walked past it he again remembered that his wife had asked him to do something for her, but he still could not think what. He walked on; but at the far end of the square, still no calmer than when he had begun his walk, a craving for peace made him retrace his steps to the door carved with crosses. The morning mass had ended a long time before and the church was empty, its cool darkness infused with the smells of frankincense and wood wax. He took a seat, intending to consider his options, but the austere surroundings were meant to inspire one to ponder eternity, not the impenetrable mysteries of loans, covenants and bankruptcies. After a while he took a book out of his pocket and began to read.

Reading helped him forget his visit to the shipping agent and he read until he lost track of time, drawn into the vortex of the story from which he only emerged, breathless and startled, when something brushed against his shoes. It was a mop: the cleaning woman had come in without him noticing and was giving him to understand that he was not welcome in the house of the Lord. He stopped mid-sentence, put the book in his pocket and left the church. The wind had died down, the waves were smaller, and with the sun still out it was not as cold. The solitude of the church had helped. He felt better in body and spirit, and an involuntary optimism crept up on him, convincing him, with fragile certainty, that everything would be fine after all. On the small balconies of whitewashed houses with blue shutters, bed linen left out to air flapped. A horse cart clip-clopped past the sole bus on the island parked at the square. He took the road out of town.

It was a long walk before the large tent with the faded red and white stripes came into view. It was called The Grand

Circus of the Orient, although not one of the thirty-odd hands and performers who worked for it had ever set foot in Asia nor had any intention of going. In fact, the isolated island on the eastern border of the country where they were now stranded while Damianos's creditors demanded their money back was the nearest they had ever come to the fabled continent. Only a few of the animals—like the Bengal tiger he had had to let go, the red and green Moluccan king parrot that could say a few words in the language of Homer, and the female elephant—were genuine natives of the East, whom the whirlwinds of destiny, or simple human cruelty, had swept away from the humid forests of their birth and condemned to perform in a bankrupt provincial circus.

When he looked in the mirror Damianos saw a man of another era—a von Humboldt or Magellan or, even, Galileo—who had lived long enough to fall behind the times. In truth he was not that old, but knew that the days when the circus was popular were gone for ever. Yet, despite the fact that his show no longer had aspirations of greatness, he believed there was still some life left in it, enough to see him to retirement. He thought that his doubts were well hidden from his staff under his velvet ringmaster's suit, not realising that a keen eye easily noticed the fraying cuffs of his jacket, the peeling felt of his hat and the scuffed toes of his boots.

When he reached the site he brought the zebras a few bales of hay and water, helped the man who was cleaning the aviary, and resumed his contemplative walk. The elephant was not in the camp. His wife was the animal's keeper and he assumed that she had gone to fetch her, but when he climbed into their caravan he found her asleep in bed with a towel over her eyes. He went to get Shanti himself. He knew where to find her. Around her neck she wore a heavy bell cast in solid bronze and the wind carried its chiming over now as the man approached the beach. He followed the sound through the trees and saw her standing near the water, which was strange because he knew that she did not like the sea. When he came closer he saw, concealed until then behind Shanti's large body, a man and a boy, both clothed, standing knee-deep in the water. The man began to shout at Damianos, but it took the ringmaster a while to understand that in his heavily accented English the man was calling for help.

'Come here, Shanti,' Damianos called. 'Leave them alone.' The elephant turned around and walked docilely towards him. 'You can come out,' he said to the man. 'She won't hurt you. She's used to people.'

He patted Shanti's trunk and called out at the man and the boy several more times before he succeeded in convincing them to come out of the water. They stood on the beach, keeping their distance from the animal, shivering in their soaked clothes. The man was barefoot, too. 'How did you get here?' Damianos asked.

'In a boat,' the foreign man said. 'Do you have water?'

'What boat?' He could not see any boat on the beach.

'It sank. We had to swim. Where can we get some water? We haven't had anything to drink in two days. The boy—'

"Is he your son?' Damianos asked the other man, again in English.

27

The boy stood close to the man and stared at the elephant warily. The man shook his head. 'No, no… Has anyone else arrived?'

'Arrived? You mean of your people? No one has arrived. Well, I don't think so. I would've heard, I'm sure. This is a small place. Your boats never come here. This place is too far. There are other islands much closer to the coast. How on earth did you get here? Were you lost?'

'Please, we need water.'

'Yes, yes. Water, right. There isn't any around here. Better come with me.'

At the camp he gave them water, took the elephant to her enclosure and tied a chain round her ankle, then led the man and boy to an empty caravan. Inside there was a pair of beds with bare mattresses fixed on opposite walls, a table with a single plastic chair, and a dusty kitchenette with a hob and sink. 'I'm afraid the kitchen is useless,' Damianos said. 'This caravan has no electricity or water. I may be able to run a cable from the generator but there's nothing I can do for the water. You can use the staff facilities. Come to get pillows and blankets.'

The man said something to the boy in their language and the boy stayed behind. Damianos walked with the man to his own caravan, where his wife was still in bed. The sound of the door did not cause any reaction from her, but the sound of more than one pair of feet on the metal floor made her pull the towel from her eyes.

'This gentleman needs somewhere to stay,' her husband announced. 'He's with a boy. I found them on the beach where Shanti goes.'

The woman's eyes turned from him to the stranger. 'Are they all right?'

'He speaks English. He says their boat capsized in the storm yesterday. I thought they could stay in the empty caravan.'

She flashed a brief smile in their visitor's direction. 'You are welcome here,' she said in English.

'Thank you.' The man looked shyly away.

Damianos said, 'They need blankets and pillows. And a pair of shoes for him.'

Mokdad stood uncomfortably at the door, barefoot, his clothes still wet, fighting back a sense of humiliation. How easily he had crossed from respectability to begging for food and shelter. He was educated, well off, he had been esteemed, and now this: nameless, homeless, an alien, an intruder. Even speaking in another language, despite the fact that he was fluent in it, felt like a weakness. Pride flared in him as he told himself he was not like anybody else in that boat, he had very little in common with any of them, he was—better. Had he made the wrong decision by leaving home? he asked himself not for the first time since the start of his journey, and a doubt greater than before weighed him down. But the fear of death was gone, that much he had achieved, and to a coward like him, he argued, this was all that really mattered. He asked, 'How can we get to the mainland from here?'

'There is a ferry,' the woman said. 'It doesn't come often out of season. It might come next week or might not, depending on the weather.' Then she noticed the water dripping from his clothes and told her husband something in their language. Mokdad put on the shoes given to him, which turned out to be too big, took the pile of blankets, sheets and pillows, also some clean clothes, thanked the man in a manner that even he himself thought half-hearted, and walked back to the caravan where Jamil was waiting. Fatigue came over him and he dropped, without bothering to make his bed, on to the old mattress. Pleasure spread down his body as he stretched out and he mumbled to the boy, who was watching him from the only chair, to have a rest too.

He thought again of the waves, the upturned dinghy, the floating luggage, the people in the water and the man in the life-jacket holding on to him. He could not sleep. He opened his eyes and for the first time took a good look at the boy standing at the window. He was around ten, with dark eyes and hair and a gaunt, sullen face. He was staring out of the window, occasionally glancing shyly at the man in bed. The next time he turned away from the window Jamil asked, 'Are you asleep, Uncle?'

It was a very long time since anyone had called him 'uncle'. They had all known he was a doctor where he lived and that was how they would address him, young and old. He said, 'Aren't you tired? You need to rest.'

'I can't sleep.'

'Make your bed,' Mokdad said, pointing at the folded bed linen. 'We can stay here for as long as we like. It's going to be fine. They're good people. They'll look after us.'

Jamil looked at him with doubt. 'The man...is he the boss here?'

'Yes, I think so. He has a wife.'

'Do you trust them?'

'Trust them?' The doctor wondered what the boy thought of him. He did not seem to be afraid of him, a murderer. Then something flickered in the boy's eyes. Mokdad could swear it was almost admiration. 'There is nothing to trust them with,' Mokdad said. 'We haven't done anything wrong. Just passing through. You don't need to worry. Get some sleep. I'll ask them for something to eat when I get up. Are you hungry?'

'No, not much.'

'Still, you have to eat. Your clothes are wet. They gave me clean ones. They're too big for you, but you'd better change.'

Jamil blushed and patted his clothes: the prospect of having to undress in front of the man filled him with dread. 'No, no, I'm fine. They're almost dry. I'm not cold.' He asked eagerly, 'What did you tell them?'

'What do you mean? I didn't tell them anything. They didn't ask me much. Don't worry. They're good people. We'll be gone in a few days. We'll take the next ferry.'

'What did you tell them about me?' Jamil insisted.

The doctor was taken aback by the question. He said, 'I said we were together in the boat.'

'Tell them you are my father.'

'Why? I've already told the man we aren't family.'

'You did? Why?' He was upset. 'You shouldn't have said that.'

'They won't tell anyone. Who would they tell? And if they do it won't make any difference. You don't need to be afraid. No one's going to send you back.'

Jamil stared at him. If that had been admiration in his eyes before, it was all gone now, its place taken over by reproach. Mokdad felt as if he had been disloyal to him. He asked, 'Where *is* your father?'

The boy shrugged and asked, 'Will you tell everyone you're my father from now on?'

'I don't understand why... Well, fine. If you like. Until we leave.'

'No, no. Until we get to the place we're going.'

Jamil waited for an answer but Mokdad said nothing. The boy said, 'Let me travel with you.'

'I can't look after you. I won't sign any papers. I won't lie to the police about it.'

'No. Just don't tell the people we come across, if they ask.'

'Fine. I'll do it. Now let me sleep. You go to bed, too. You need rest, Jamil.'

He took one of the blankets and covered himself. He thought that he ought not have spoken to the child like that, he should have been kinder to him. Jamil had not said anything unreasonable: his family was gone and he needed someone. He was only a little boy.

Jamil watched him, pleased that the man had agreed. The idea had come to him on the upturned dinghy but he had not dared suggest it until they were safe. He was happy now, so happy to know that they would be together from now on. He would not have to keep his promise to part from Mokdad at the end of their journey. There was bound to be a way to make him change his mind and stay together afterwards, too.

He wanted to see the elephant again, and when Mokdad fell asleep he went out. There were several people around, working, paying no attention to him. That was how it normally was: he was invisible to the grown-ups unless he did something of which they disapproved. They thought of him as little and immature but he felt neither weak nor foolish. He thought with satisfaction how he was still alive when everyone else in the boat had drowned. Who was the weak one now? The fact that the man had helped him did not lessen the magnitude of his achievement: he had stayed afloat, he had felt no fear. He thought of his saviour again. He was not like other men. Jamil was moved at the thought of how Mokdad had held him in his arms on the upturned boat, keeping him warm, staying awake all night and letting him sleep. He did not know why that had made him weep when it happened but at least the man had not seen him. He didn't want Mokdad to think of him as a little boy who cried.

He found the elephant in its enclosure, tied by the leg to a tree with a chain that seemed too flimsy for it. He stepped back when the animal turned its head to look at him. He screamed, a loud cry at the top of his lungs, to get a reaction from it, and it annoyed him that the animal's placid gaze did not change. He had never seen any exotic animal in real life, only in books and the occasional television programme. He thought of his sisters, who would let him watch television when their mother was out. How he missed them… He had seen what had happened to them: Mokdad had wanted to save them, but the other one in the life-jacket had held him back. He was glad his friend had killed him; he admired him for it.

Someone spoke to him in the foreign language. It was the man who had brought them there, the one who must own the circus. Jamil, who spoke no other language than his mother tongue, blushed. The man waved him over and he went to him unwillingly, vaguely expecting to be slapped or punished in some other way for something; he was not aware of having done anything wrong but that was how grown-ups always behaved. The circus owner began to gesture and laugh and Jamil now thought, with another rush of blood to his face, that he was making fun of him. All he wanted was to go back to the caravan and be with Mokdad. But he did not dare walk away. His mind was full of suspicion: he feared the circus owner might take offence and throw the two of them out. Still talking in his incomprehensible language, the circus owner put his hand in his pocket and gave him a banknote. Jamil was surprised but took it without hesitation, placing his hand across his chest and giving a slight bow.

He was disappointed to find the doctor still asleep when he returned to the caravan. He wanted to show him the money and tell him what had happened. He sat down on the bed across from him, trying not to make any noise. It was hard to stay still. He was always restless; even now that he was very tired from everything that had happened to them, his mind had to be occupied with something and his body pulsed with an energy he could not quite control. Sometimes he felt there was an adversary inside him with whom he fought but mostly could not subdue—he would often let him take charge and he, Jamil, the boy he saw in the mirror, would follow with a sense of dread. Those instances, when he did not quite know what he was doing, why he was doing it or what the outcome of his actions would be, were the most exciting ones: fear and a sense of malice eased the boredom from which he suffered like a disease.

He took off his shoes and bashfully lay down next to Mokdad in the narrow bed, covering himself with the same blanket carefully so that their bodies did not touch, and drifted off to a happy sleep, thinking how when he woke up he would give the money to Mokdad. If he refused it, he, Jamil, would insist, would say that it was for both of them now that they were together for ever.

Three

DARKNESS FELL, the generator droned, and a few lights flickered in the caravans parked in a row at the far end of the camp. Damianos walked towards them with his hands in the pockets of his overalls. The dozen caravans housed his wife and him, the circus hands, a family of aerialists, a contortionist, an ageing clown, a magician, and the few animal tamers who were in charge of the last animals: several exotic birds, six zebras, four poodles and an Indian macaque (he led the elephant act himself).

Beyond the fields overgrown with wild thorn bushes, a strip of red light was all that separated the earth from the sky. Outside his caravan he took off his overalls and threw them into an old oil drum. He made little noise but the front door creaked and a torch lit him up. 'It's only me,' he said, offering his habitual greeting in a flat voice and without much longing for coming home, to confirm, like every evening at the same time, that he was not an unexpected visitor, which had never been the case, or, just as unlikely so far from the town, a prowler. He did not believe he was being unreasonable to suspect, with near certainty, that the only purpose of that daily ritual of the suddenly opened door, the flash of the torch and the silence was to make him feel unwelcome.

The woman went back inside and returned with a steaming kettle, a box of powder detergent and a towel. He washed his hands in the torchlight, letting out little exclamations of pain every time the boiling water splashed against his skin. Somewhere in another caravan someone laughed, the zebras snorted in the cold evening and the smell of turpentine on the discarded overalls in the drum spread in the air.

It was a big caravan, whose furniture was meant to offer the comforts of home except that an upright piano took too much space. It was an extravagance that might have seemed justified in happier times but it had been silent for several years, an undisturbed veil of dust covering its fallboard. The ringmaster sat at the kitchen table and said with mock exuberance, 'My, oh, my, what a long day.'

He felt alone when he came back in the evenings, but not as lonely as late at night when he lay a few inches away from his wife in bed. If by accident, in their random movements during sleep, one of them happened to touch the other with an inert hand, a foot or an elbow, the other's body, used to its solitude, quickly sensed the unconscious intimacy and instinctively, in the midst of its sleep, moved away from the intruder, rejecting the warmth or coldness or clamminess of the foreign skin and shrinking back to the edge of the bed. In the morning the strip of no-man's-land between the couple was still cool and dry, and neither could quite recall exactly what had happened. Only a few times a year, which were becoming rarer, was the gap crossed by one or the other of them during the night, and, fully awake but not in full command of their senses, in pitch dark (even a drop of light was enough to foil it) they blindly made love, if that was what they called it, guided by animal instinct rather than feeling, until, relieved at last, the need that had ambushed them satisfied, they drew apart and each returned to their own side of the bed with every intention of forgetting it had ever happened—a wish denied them, to their mutual embarrassment, by the cold sweat stain on the sheet in the morning.

'The boy is nice but shy,' Damianos said. 'I gave him some money. I think you'll like him.'

'What boy?'

'The one who came with the man. Didn't I tell you he wasn't alone? The child doesn't speak a word of English but he's full of curiosity. You'll see him around tomorrow.'

'Was it just him and his father in the boat?'

'He isn't his father. He had a family but they drowned.'

'That's awful,' the woman said. She had gone back to bed and he sat at the kitchen table under a lamp that dimmed every time the voltage dropped. His wife said, 'Will they be all right in the old caravan?'

'There's nowhere else to put them.'

'Will you tell anyone?'

'Report them? What for?' Damianos said. 'Entering the country illegally? I couldn't care less about that. In any case, they'll be on their way soon.'

'I was thinking perhaps the police might help them. Give them papers, I don't know. What happens in these cases?'

'I have no idea. If they want me to, I'll take them to the police. Otherwise I won't interfere. It's not my business what they do.'

'Where are they going?'

'We didn't discuss it. I doubt if he'd tell me. The man is rather guarded. He let slip he was a doctor.'

The woman said, 'A doctor, travelling like that. Did you speak to the priest?'

'The priest? What do you mean? About them?' Then Damianos remembered what his wife had asked him to do in town that morning. Of course; the priest... He felt no regret for having forgotten. 'I was busy with Rajanya and it slipped my mind,' he said. 'They would've dropped him in the water if I hadn't been there. I'd do it tomorrow but since I have no urgent business in town why don't you go and speak to the kind Father yourself?'

'Don't you want to have the memorial service?'

'I didn't say I don't want to. We can have it if you wish. Personally, I don't need a priest to remind me of my daughter.'

She shook her head with disdain. Having that sort of conversation with him was a daily habit, as though its purpose was for them both to spend their venom before sharing a bed. She lay on the fringe of the glow of the dim light, the poison coming out drop by drop in silence. It was almost painful to look at her even in the dark, like staring at a harsh electric light. His eyes lingered on her silhouette and he wondered, as he had done many times since their daughter's death, what was stopping her from leaving him. Perhaps she took too much pleasure in punishing him with her presence or maybe she could not leave: they were fused together by tragedy for ever, like a couple buried in the ashes of Pompeii. It was dark outside the window. He could hear the generator droning and the animals shuffling about in their enclosures. He said, 'You won't find Anna in a church. She's not there. She is,' he said bluntly, 'nowhere.'

But it was a lie. The girl was everywhere: in the circus tent and at the town, a pale face across the street and a shadow in the caravan. She had died that morning on the quay where he had seen a girl who looked a little like her, and she would die again the next time he saw another who resembled her in some slight detail—a smile, a stare or something about the way she skipped along, flashes of memory that briefly jolted him out of his grief before plunging him deeper in it.

The woman said, 'I hate your good sense.'

His good sense, he thought with sarcasm. Had it been five years already? The circus had been on tour, the girl had been riding alone, she had fallen off the cremello and broken her neck. She had been eleven years old—eleven! Letting her ride unsupervised so young... They should have known better. His good sense.

His wife said from the bed, 'There is a letter for you. On top of the piano.'

He picked up the envelope, guessing the sender before looking at the postmark. He tore it open and his eyes scanned the lines hastily: *In reply to your recent letter...* The lightbulb almost went out and he waited for the power to return, then read on: *Unfortunately, after careful review of your application...* The writing blurred before his eyes. He stood holding the letter, his initial sense of hope having turned into mild disappointment. It was fitting to suffer. If the answer had been positive he might have felt happy, and he could never be happy again, not after what had happened to his daughter. He neatly folded back the letter under his wife's distant stare. She said coolly, 'Well, are they going to extend the loan?'

'No.'

'What did they say?'

'To pass on their regards to my lovely wife.'

The concern went from her face and she became her usual self again, harsh and unrelenting. He almost envied her: if only he could have that kind of strength too, but he could find no one to hate with conviction other than himself, which gave him no strength at all; rather, it made him weaker. He heard her saying, 'I suppose you could always try another bank.'

'There's no point,' he said, and hid the letter in his pocket. 'That was the third one. The reasons for refusing are always the same.' His eyes took in the crammed interior of the caravan and a pang of dislike for the piano stirred in him. He aimed his resentment towards it, saying, 'That thing takes an awful lot of room.'

'What, the piano? I don't see why it bothers you so much,' the woman said, complacently. 'You're hardly ever here to notice.'

'We don't even know if it still works.'

'The salty air certainly hasn't done it any good.'

'What are you keeping it for, then? Why don't you throw it away, for God's sake?'

'It isn't in a bad condition, it just needs a few simple things done to it and to be tuned. There is no one who knows how to fix it here.'

'If you won't play it,' he said tetchily, 'what's the use?'

The woman said, 'I have no intention of playing it. I would like to have it fixed and sell it. We could use the money, couldn't we? There is a woman in town who's very keen to have it for her music classes. She says she's willing to buy it if it gets fixed.'

'How much would you get?'

'Not enough to pay our debts.'

'I'm not going to pay for a repair man to come all this way if it isn't worth it.'

Truce struck at the arranged time, just before midnight, to their mutual secret relief even though they knew it would be broken at first light. Thunder crashed and it began to rain instantly and heavily. The cold eased and the air through the gap in the window began to smell of earth and dung. The lightbulb went out while the storm raged. The lights in the other caravans had gone out, too; the whole camp was in the dark: the generator had shut down. There was no reason to fix it so late at night, Damianos decided; he would do it in the morning. Besides, it was good to be in the dark, it made him feel safe. Darkness hid him from some threat he could not define. You stopped caring much about things you could not see: people's reactions, your own face... There was a certain—honesty, he supposed, about it; you could be true to yourself in the dark. Perhaps blindness was like that. It was coming into the light that bothered him, when he was expected to behave a certain way. He could not be unhappy among other people; he had to become someone else, an actor coming on stage.

He took the letter out of his pocket and went to the window where in the light from the moon he could just make out the sentences. In the otherwise typed letter, *Dear Damianos* and *Sincerely yours* were written by hand, in the rushed friendliness of a busy man. He had a nodding acquaintance with the bank manager; it was why he had written to him directly, hoping it would make a difference. He tore it up quietly and put the pieces back in his pocket while the rain rapped against the steel roof and streamed down the window.

The woman pulled the blanket over herself. It was too dark to see him; she only heard his feet at the other end of the caravan. Hatred stirred in her at the thought of him, but she did not wallow in it; she was so tired tonight. She waited for the rain to stop: she liked to sleep with the windows open. She thought of the piano, which she had bought to teach Anna to play. She remembered sitting with her and showing her the basic chords; the girl's small hands on the ivory keys… They had only had a few weeks of lessons before she'd had the accident. It had happened so fast, so simply, like snuffing a candle. The rain tapped against the window, keeping time like the pendulum of a clock; she could not bear listening to it. She reached out of the blanket and took two sleeping pills with water. The piano, she thought, lying back in bed; no, she would not get rid of it. It was out of the question.

Four

THE ELEPHANT approached her with slow steps and felt the woman's face with her trunk. There was something childlike about the animal's need to touch her that reminded Olga of her daughter. The trunk withdrew shyly and the animal stood there looking at her, enormous and at the same time vulnerable in the human world: too big to hide, nowhere to run away to, trapped in a place where her size was not enough to protect her. Olga was grateful to her. Shanti's silent companionship had nursed her through her grief and back to a state that resembled a normal life.

She had no doubts about the animal's intelligence and had grown to dislike watching her performances. The sight of an elephant balancing on a ball or seated on her haunches with her front legs raised in the air or performing a handstand saddened her, her sole comfort the hope that the animal saw the whole thing as a game and was not hurt but looked after well.

They left the camp and slowly walked across the fields, the woman in a pair of long rubber boots and a raincoat, the elephant's feet brushing against the thorn bushes and coming down delicately on the wet earth. It had rained all night but the soil was hard and stony and there was very little mud. The earth was barren across the whole island where only bushes, wildflowers and a few pines and almond trees grew. On the hills away from the coast there were no roads or houses, and those were good places to take the elephant for a walk and to find food. But there was not all that much grass and every day Olga had to walk with Shanti a little farther away from the campsite to find enough food so that now, several months after they had come to the island, they had to walk quite far, beyond the hills she could see from the camp.

That morning they took another direction altogether, one they had not gone along before, but it was still a while before they found enough grass for the animal to start grazing. While Shanti ate, Olga walked around by herself. She did not stray too far, mindful of the animal, who occasionally paused in pulling up the grass with her trunk, lifted her head and looked around, checking that her keeper was still there. Olga climbed to the top of the nearest hill, staying within sight of the elephant, and looked around. The hills were studded with wild bushes, a few clusters of trees, a rock projecting vertically from the ground like a prehistoric monument. Her eyes swept across the familiar landscape and stopped at an unexpected form some distance away. It was a small whitewashed church built so far from the town that it would only be visited a couple of times a year. It was made of stone and covered in rough plaster, had an arched roof but no bell. There would be no use for it: no one lived for miles around. A church without a priest or parish; she was glad to have discovered it. The only light came through a door so small that she had to bend her head to enter. The walls were unadorned and the only piece of furniture was a simple table covered with a plastic cloth on which stood the framed picture of a saint and a vigil lamp, which was, surprisingly, burning. She went back out into the light.

Behind the church the sloping ground concealed a terraced hillside where a small cemetery had been built. Among its handful of stone crosses, an old woman dressed in black was on her knees and was pulling up the overgrown grass from a grave with a concentration that for a while kept her unaware of Olga's presence. Finally she raised her head, nodded at Olga unsmilingly and returned to her task. Once she had rid the small plot of weeds she washed the cross with a brush, dipping it in a bucket of soapy water. The inscription cut in the cross bore the name of a man who had died in middle age several years before—a husband or a brother, given the woman's age. The shining sun of a moment earlier was being fast shrouded in blue-grey clouds. Olga thought that she ought to go but lingered on, fascinated by the older woman, who must have believed in an afterlife—what other reason would compel her to come all that way? For Olga it was impossible to think of her daughter as anything more than a memory trapped in her mind.

The wind was picking up. 'It's going to rain,' Olga said, but the other woman did not raise her head. There was a crash of thunder, but the old woman's brush went on scrubbing the indelible lichen on the stone with the same doggedness. Olga said again, 'Come. We'll go together.' This time the woman waved her away with annoyance. It was a long walk back and they would have to set off now to have any chance of avoiding the rain. But Olga was reluctant to go, kept there by an unreasonable responsibility to the woman. It was sad seeing her struggle like that: she had been scrubbing for a while, but hardly any lichen had come off. Olga could not watch her any more. She snatched the brush from her hand, knelt down and began to scrub the stone hard herself, pausing only to dip the brush in the bucket. The other woman looked on in astonishment but did not object: she must have been quite tired already and grateful for the help.

The first drops of rain spurred Olga to scrub faster, determined to finish her task quickly and walk with the woman back to the camp. Soon it was raining properly but Olga kept on scrubbing. After a few more minutes she paused and looked at the stone, which was not much cleaner than before. The rain was falling harder now and she took off her raincoat and put it over the woman's shoulders, then went back to her task, working with rage while the rain soaked through her clothes. She did not know what had come over her. She was angry at the storm and the stone cross, which she could not clean; she was angry at whoever was buried under it; she was angry at the old woman.

She was shivering and there was no sign of the rain stopping. Shanti trumpeted: she was looking for her. Olga could not stay any longer, she had to leave. If she were on her own... But she had to find more food for the animal and they had to get back; they had come quite far from the camp. She stopped, breathing heavily, her wet hair plastered to her head, and wiped the rain from her face. She was not angry any more, just felt weak and foolish, wondering what on earth she was doing. She threw the brush in the bucket and told the woman, 'Come. Now we have to go,' but the other gave her back the raincoat and stayed where she was. 'No, no. Keep it,' Olga said. The woman shook her head and mumbled something incomprehensible before taking the brush from the bucket and kneeling at the grave. Olga climbed the hill back towards the church. On the top she turned and gave the woman on the terraced hill a last look. There she still was scrubbing away at the cross, a small black figure in the driving rain. The elephant stood some distance away from the church, pulling out grass. Shanti came towards her and they walked in the direction they had come from earlier.

The rain eased but did not stop, the cold wind from the sea was still blowing in gusts, and Olga thought of the old woman at the grave, the rain soaking through her black cotton dress. She walked faster with her head down to avoid the rain that the wind blew in her face, paying little attention to the direction they were going. She thought that she knew how to get back and for a while she recognised various places they had passed on their way to the small church on the hill—the upright rock, a deep gully, a collapsed dry stone wall—but after a few more minutes of brisk walking, when she raised her head and squinted through the rain again, she saw no landmark in any direction. All hills looked the same on the island: she should not worry, she was going the right way. She searched for the tallest hill around to try to orientate herself, and headed towards it. From its top she could see the sea very far away, but neither the camp nor the town because there were still taller hills farther away, blocking her view of a large part of the island. Her destination could be behind any of them; there was no way of knowing.

She whistled at the elephant to follow her and now headed towards the nearest of those higher hills, which was still some distance away. The steep hillside was covered with scree and Olga slipped back several times, once sliding down a long way before managing to break her fall by grabbing hold of an exposed root. She stood up, her clothes muddied, her hands badly scratched, and resumed her climb. A great disappointment met her at the top: she could still not see the campsite. She had to try another hill. Coming down was even harder, slowly walking backwards, which took a long time and left her out of breath.

The next hill was taller but not as steep and she decided to use the animal to get to the top. She had Shanti kneel and she sat on the animal's neck and led her on. But after a few steps Shanti refused to climb any more. Olga, tired, cold, the rain coming down, urged Shanti on, speaking to her, but still the animal refused to move. Olga thought she was going to get a bad cold; Shanti was thirsty, and they had to cross several hills to get back. Everything filled the woman with anger: her frustration, her fingers going numb, her runny nose, the enormous unyielding animal. She kept tapping Shanti with her stick, kicking her heels against the animal's sides and calling at her to move, but the elephant backed off from the hillside and trumpeted. It was the first time since Olga had become her keeper that she had refused her commands. She understood that the animal was afraid of climbing the hillside because it was slippery or would tire her or perhaps she did not like heights, but she knew that she could do it, just that one time, and she would be doing a favour to both of them.

Olga, her mind filled with thoughts of defeat and helplessness, began to hit Shanti, determined to make her do what she wanted. The stick broke but the elephant still did not move. Shaken by rage, she dug its splintered end in the soft flesh behind the animal's ear. Shanti made a loud noise and began to walk. Olga guided her uphill with her voice and little kicks of her heels, the blood on the wrinkled brown skin smearing her trousers as she sat astride the animal's neck. Her rage spent, she regretted

hurting her; she had never hurt her before. It was difficult
to explain to herself why she had done it. At least there
was no one around and she could hold back her shame.
She would tell no one. She led Shanti uphill on a zigzag
path but did not hurry her, letting her choose her pace.
Among the loose stones and mud only the thorny bushes
gave the animal a firm foothold, but even then her
enormous weight often uprooted them and she had to stop
and steady herself not to slip.

It was taking them a long time to reach the top. It was
almost midday, they had been gone for several hours and
the church was a white speck behind them. Could they
have come so far and still be such a long way from the
camp? As they climbed higher they exposed themselves
more to the wind, and the rain fell against Olga's face as
hard as hail. She held on to the elephant, who swayed and
slipped but kept climbing, the slow rumble of Shanti's
heart rippling through the large body, the hard loose skin
under Olga's legs stretching with each laboured breath,
and she thought that they could not go back now, they
were almost there. She would never force Shanti to do
anything like that again.

The wind on the hilltop almost threw her off the animal,
but the view through squinting eyes allayed her fears. At
last she could see, even though it was still very far, the
circus camp. Now she worried about climbing down the
hill, how to guide Shanti along a safe path. Looking back
where they had climbed from, she realised the enormity
of what she had forced the elephant to do. She got off
her and patted her on the trunk, but could tell the animal

was sullen. She did not flap her ears or make any sound; her trunk hung limply down. Shanti could kill Olga if she wanted to, very easily: all she had to do was grab hold of her with her trunk and crush her under her body. It was only friendship that was stopping her—or maybe a broken spirit and the fear of more pain.

Olga let her rest before they set off. Even though she led her along a path with a gentle slope and the firmest ground, the elephant, unnerved by the height, struggled to follow her. With the woman urging her on and at the same time trying to calm her down they made very slow progress, but at least the rain had stopped and the hill on that side gave them shelter from the wind. Olga looked at the camp in the far distance with the big tent pitched in the middle and her thoughts turned to her husband. He might be working somewhere over there at that moment; there was always something that needed repair and they could not afford to replace anything. Or he might have gone to the town again, secretly from her, he thought, to try to get a loan from somebody. In truth when he was not around she felt sorry for him, but her pity vanished as soon as she saw him again. The thought that he was there comforted her, but she also suffered from his close presence, his talking to her, the sound of his footsteps, the rustle of the newspaper, his breathing when he slept, all the unintentional sounds that broke the benevolent illusion of her solitude.

They were halfway down the hill when the elephant slipped. Olga was walking ahead when Shanti lost her footing and fell on her side, then tumbled to the foot of the hill, a long way down, knocking herself against rocks and bushes as she went. By the time Olga reached her the animal was back on her feet, but there was a large bleeding cut on her leg. The woman tried to examine it but Shanti turned away from her. The animal's fear of her shamed her and she did not attempt to touch her again, just called at her to follow her, and they made the rest of the walk along an easier but longer path, arriving at the camp late in the afternoon. Shanti's wound was still bleeding. Olga needed help but was told that her husband had gone to the town.

She remembered that the foreigner who was staying with them was a doctor and knocked on the door of his caravan. A voice said something in another language, which she assumed to be a permission to enter, but when she came in she found him in bed. He quickly pushed off his blanket and got up. It was cold in the caravan and he had been lying in his clothes.

Olga said, 'Oh, excuse me. Am I bothering you?' and felt shy. His hair was uncombed, his clothes wrinkled and he had not shaved since he had come but he smelt of soap. There was a large plastic basin on the floor and she imagined him standing in it and awkwardly washing himself before putting her husband's clothes on.

'No, no. I just thought it was the boy,' Mokdad said. 'He's gone out.'

'I could come back later.'

'No, please stay. I lie in bed all day. Nothing else to do.'

'It is very cold in here.'

'Oh, I don't mind,' he said, 'I'm used to it.' He had on

the same light jacket that he had worn when her husband had first brought him to the camp. He was trying to stop himself from trembling, as if it would have seemed ungrateful to feel cold. 'Is there anything…?'

'Hasn't my husband reconnected the electricity yet?' Olga asked. 'He had it disconnected from the generator when the man who stayed here left. I'm very sorry. I'll tell him to connect you back.'

'I haven't seen him in a while,' Mokdad said, making his bed hurriedly. 'Could I speak to him now? I don't mind the cold myself, but maybe for the sake of the child…'

'He's gone to town. I'll tell him when he gets back.'

'Thank you.' He added reassuringly, 'We won't be here for much longer.'

'Stay as long as you want to. How's the boy? I've seen him around but I think he's avoiding me. I think he's avoiding everyone.'

'Has he done anything bad? He doesn't speak English.'

'No, no. It's just that he goes near the animals a lot. He needs to be careful.'

'I apologise. I didn't know.'

'Oh, I didn't mean… He's done nothing bad,' Olga said. 'I'm just worried. Those are wild animals.' And she thought of Shanti and how she, Olga, had hurt the elephant more than the elephant would ever hurt her.

'I will talk to him.'

His firm tone of voice worried her. She said, 'Don't tell him off, please. He's welcome to go anywhere he likes. He can watch the animals but from a little distance, that's all. I don't want anything to happen to him.'

He nodded at the floor. Olga wondered whether it had sounded like a reproach. She said, 'I've come to ask you a favour.'

He looked up eagerly. 'Yes. Tell me. What can I do?'

'Is it true you are a doctor?'

She could feel him going stiff, as if he was expecting to be accused of something, and she rushed to say, 'Our elephant had an accident. A deep cut on her leg. She hasn't had any injury before and I hardly know what to do.'

'Hadn't you better ask a vet?'

'There isn't one on the island. My husband looks after the animals when they get sick, but who knows when he'll get back.' He did not say anything and she added, 'It was my fault. I'd rather not tell him, you know.'

Now that she was asking for his help she could see him calming down and a sense of pride flickering in his face. He no longer looked haggard. She could imagine him walking hurriedly into a ward ahead of a flock of nurses, his white coat flapping behind him, asking questions in a clipped voice. A person had no fixed qualities; it all depended on the circumstances. She said, 'I don't think it's very serious. But you never know.'

'Very well,' Mokdad said. 'Will the animal let me come near?'

'I will be there with you. Don't worry, she's very well behaved. She trusts me.'

He stayed behind the steel fence while she entered the enclosure and brought Shanti over. He examined the wound, which was still bleeding, and announced that the muscle was not damaged but nevertheless the cut was very deep and had to be stitched. He asked her for boiled water and iodine, and, if she had chamomile, to make as much infusion as she could. He cleaned the dirt off the wound with the water, bathed it in the chamomile and stitched it as best he could, using fishing line and a large hook from which he had cut off the barb.

She watched him with curiosity. He had an Arab face—the way she understood it from film and television—with an olive complexion, long nose, and dark eyes made more distinctive by black eyebrows. He worked with absolute concentration, his skilled fingers covered with blood, his lips set in a thoughtful pout. In all likelihood he was younger than she was, but nothing about him offered any clue as to whether he was married or had a family. There was no wedding ring—did they wear one where he came from? It was unlikely that he was Christian but she did ask him, having to repeat the question to get his attention. He chuckled and shook his head to deny it without looking away from his task.

Mokdad finished sewing the wound and cleaned it one last time with iodine. While he was washing his hands with the water left in the bucket, she led the elephant back to the middle of the enclosure and tied its leg to the tree with the chain. Before he left, the woman thanked him, offering her hand. She seemed sincerely grateful, but the gesture struck him as awkward and formal or done distractedly and he was disappointed not to have earned, as far as he could tell, her admiration. Even though he was not particularly proud of his profession he had tried to impress her with his expertise, but she had made him feel ill at ease. As soon as the animal was not bleeding, the woman's tense expression had given way to her habitual unemotional contemplation.

He was glad to return to his caravan and his dusty bed, but a moment later he could not resist the urge to sit up and part the frayed curtains to search for her. She was still standing with the elephant in the middle of the enclosure where she had been when he left them. He thought that perhaps she was talking to the animal, he could not tell from that distance, but then her shoulders began to shake as though she was sobbing. All the while the elephant stood perfectly still, and the way that she leant against the animal made her seem from the distance, he thought, like a penitent about to prostrate herself to the effigy of a primitive god.

Five

A COLD WIND fluttered the candy-striped walls of the circus tent, rocked the caravans and swirled a cloud of dust and grit around the camp, blinding animals and people. At midday, the wind still blowing, a heavy rain began to hammer down on to the caravan roofs and turned the well-trodden ground to mud. To shelter the animals from the storm the circus hands took them to the big tent, which soon resembled Noah's ark. Only the elephant was left out in the thunderstorm, pacing her enclosure as far as the length of her chain would allow, her feet splashing in the mud, the water streaming down her body, occasionally raising her head to drink the rain.

It rained most days. The camp was often flooded and the doctor stayed in the caravan with Jamil. They still waited for the ferry to come. He lay in bed trying to avoid the boy's stare and bringing to mind the hospital where he had worked. His daily ward rounds, his white coat, his patients: he had abandoned everything that had given him a sense of pride and kept him happy for so long. He had been operating on men wounded in battle without ever questioning his commitment to his job, then the ward had begun to fill with civilians caught up in the fighting. It was when the little children had started to come in that he had felt the utter absurdity of the war. He had fled when he was most desperately needed... Again he wondered whether he had made the wrong choice and was now being punished for it, trapped on an isolated island to which he did not belong any more than the circus animals.

When the wind and rain eased, at around two in the afternoon, he escaped his shelter, stopping Jamil from following him with an impatient wave of his hand and the excuse that he had some business to attend to in the town when, in truth, he simply wanted to be left alone. He resented the boy's attachment to him and he resented his own sense of responsibility towards him even though he had argued with himself several times against the need to do anything more than make sure Jamil got on the ship to the mainland. But he had promised to stay with him until the end of their journey and he ought to keep his word.

One night the noise of the rain, or maybe it had been the cold, had woken him up from a deep sleep and he had found Jamil lying asleep next to him. He had shaken the boy awake, and Jamil had mumbled with sullen embarrassment that he was afraid of thunder, but he'd sent him to his own bed. It had not happened again, but from then on he had been able to sense the child's disappointment. It made him feel both guilty and irritated, as if he had broken, by mistake, some tasteless ornament of little tangible value for which its owner nevertheless had great affection.

The day before the ferry was due at last, he went to see their host and broach the matter of the fare. He had been putting it off until then, hoping that the other man, who had already given Jamil some money, would offer them more without the doctor asking. He would have sent Jamil in his place but thought better of it, not trusting him with such an important mission and not wanting to be in his debt. He spied the circus owner walking alone across the camp and approached him with a serious face and a thumping heart. He had never before asked anyone for money and did not know what to say. He regretted offering his clammy hand as soon as he did, but, after pulling it back a little and seeing the bewildered look on the other man's face, he reached out again and squeezed his benefactor's confident hand with a servile bow of his head, a gesture that he had never made before either and which gave him a pang of self-loathing. To compensate for his obsequiousness he did not greet the circus owner, not even with a single word or smile, but said, 'The ferry is coming tomorrow.'

'Oh, is it?' the circus owner said, cheerfully. 'That's good news.'

'I was told by the shipping agent.'

The other man suddenly pouted. 'The shipping agent, eh? I wouldn't trust anything that man says.'

Mokdad was alarmed. 'Do you think he was lying?'

'What? Well, no... Perhaps not about that.' He smiled with an effort and patted the foreigner on the shoulder. 'Oh, forget it. It's a personal matter.'

'We have to get the tickets.'

'Today? Oh, I'm sure there'll be plenty of seats.' But he did not want to appear rude. 'Of course,' the circus owner added, 'you don't want to miss it.' He surveyed the muddy camp with a look of dejection. He said, 'The service isn't very frequent in winter. And it's a slow ship.'

Mokdad was trying to muster the courage to ask for the money when the circus owner spoke again. 'Where's your little friend? He's a good boy. Terrible what happened to him.' The doctor nodded and the other said, 'You're doing a great thing, looking after him.'

'It's only until we get—I don't have a family myself.' He should not be telling him about his intention to part from Jamil when they reached their destination. Instead he said, 'I was travelling alone. Now I need to think about him, too.'

'Oh, you should,' the circus owner said. 'Does he have family where you're going?'

'I don't think so.'

'Ah, poor boy. Losing one's family…' He shook his head ruefully and put his hand in his pocket. 'Terrible. I'm no stranger to loss myself.' He took his hand out again; it was empty. 'Excuse me. I shouldn't be bothering you with my private matters.'

'Of course if I were alone it would've been different,' Mokdad said, disappointed. 'I can take care of myself. But with the boy…'

'You've been through hell, both of you,' the other man agreed. He moved a step and his shoe landed in a muddy pool. He swore at it and said, 'I often think about it—what that child must have seen. He's lucky to have you.'

The doctor agreed politely and said, 'Now the time has come for us to leave.'

'Well, then. It's been a pleasure meeting you.'

'I wanted to speak to you before we did.'

'I hope your stay here wasn't too bad, was it? I'm sorry for the old caravan. There was nowhere else.'

'No, no, I thank you.'

'Not at all,' the circus owner said.

'I lost everything, you see. When I fell off the boat.'

'I know, you said so. A terrible thing. If there is anything…'

'In fact, I suppose… You have been very kind to us, but you see…'

'Do you have any money?'

At last, Mokdad thought with relief. 'No. All gone. At sea.' He watched the man putting his hand back in his pocket. 'You've been very kind to us.'

'How much would you need?'

'Just the fare. I don't exactly know how much the tickets are, do you? If you could come with us to the agency tomorrow and get them—'

The other shook his head vigorously. 'I'm never setting foot in that place again.'

'But I don't quite know the price.'

'Will fifty do?'

'Yes. I'm sure it's more than enough. Thank you.' Mokdad said again, 'Just enough for the tickets.'

His host took out his wallet. Mokdad watched in silence while the other man opened it like gutting a fish. He said, 'Take a hundred.'

'No, no.'

'Go on, take it. For the boy. You'll need it.' He held the money out. 'Have a safe journey.'

Mokdad looked at the money with embarrassment. Pride made him say, 'No, fifty should be enough.'

'Why not all of it? I wish I could give you more, but I have to be careful with money these days. Financial difficulties, you understand. I don't want to bore you with it.'

The doctor said firmly, 'Fifty is more than enough. Please.'

'Fine. If you insist.' The circus owner returned the rest of the banknotes into his wallet and put it back in his pocket. He took a step back: he wanted to go. He said, 'Just get on that ferry. You know, I envy you, doctor. I wish I could leave this place too. But it's impossible. If I set foot on the mainland right now I'll lose everything. Yes, I envy you. You owe nothing to anyone.'

Six

THE WEATHER WAS bad again, with the wind blowing all night, but Mokdad had no trouble falling asleep despite the cold, the air whistling through the cracks and the loose door banging. The calm of his sleep was finally broken when the memory of the sea crossing returned as an intense dream. The darkness, the storm, the other passengers, the capsized dinghy, the struggle in the water, the tailor drowning: everything felt as real as he remembered it and he tossed and turned in bed, groaning and gasping for breath. When he woke up shortly before dawn, of his own accord, the dream followed him back to consciousness and he continued to think about what had happened at sea. He wondered if he really had tried to help the man he had snatched the life-jacket from when he'd realised what he had done. He remembered doing so but was no longer sure. It felt like a story he had made up to absolve himself of guilt.

He tried not to think about it but there was little else that he could turn his mind to. The journey ahead of him, his life in another country—he no longer cared to speculate about them; instead he thought about the woman. He had been thinking about her ever since she had asked him to treat the elephant's wound. He often sat at the window of his caravan to catch a secret glimpse of her if she happened to walk across the camp, glimpses that slowly revealed, like an old painting being restored, a picture that little resembled the woman he remembered from their first meeting. Her unhappiness was still there, to be sure, but there was also a defiance about her which he had not noticed at first, even though it was not clear what or whom she defied. Death? Marriage? Her husband's circus and its workers? The world at large? He did not know but his spying on her encouraged him to believe that he could read her true emotions in what to someone else might seem an impassive face. He did not doubt his opinions of her; his conviction gave him the satisfaction that they shared, just the two of them, an intimate secret.

He was convinced that since their first meeting she had gradually been looking better. Her hair was always combed now; she was losing her pallor and would greet him when they came across each other, albeit without a smile. It was pleasant to imagine, even though he did not quite believe it, resisting the allure of such a likelihood, that he might be responsible for her transformation. What did she think of him? he began to wonder as he lay in bed waiting for dawn, until a little idea was born in him that they would meet again a year on, somewhere else, when he would not be a beggar but a respectable hospital doctor and they would become friends. It was a foolish whimsy, but he sustained it in his mind for as long as he could, savouring it like a fantasy, which one knows very well to be untrue but cannot resist the pleasure it gives.

On the day of their departure the sky was obscured by dense storm clouds and the wind, which had eased towards dawn, began to blow with great force. It was not yet time to leave for the town but the sky threatened to rain at any minute and Mokdad told Jamil to get ready. He delayed, however, by stopping at the owner's caravan across the camp. To his disappointment the man answered the door. Raising his voice as much as he reasonably could in the hope that his wife would hear, the doctor asked him to thank her on behalf of the boy and him. There was no indication that she was in, but he had a sudden suspicion that she might be lying in bed with no great wish to see him. The thought unsettled him and he lingered on his host's doorstep for the chance to disprove it, talking about anything he could think of until he became aware that he was repeating the words from the day before. He concluded his leave-taking without having put his mind at rest.

As he was about to go, the other man told him to wait. Mokdad supposed that he went inside to call his wife and he instinctively smiled in anticipation, but the circus owner returned with a large umbrella. Mokdad declined it politely and kept saying no, even when he was told that he could leave it with the owner of the coffee shop in town before boarding the ship. Finally his resistance was overcome by the first drops of rain and he accepted the umbrella with another display of obsequiousness against his will.

On the waterfront the waves crashed against the seawall and the wind almost snatched the umbrella from his hands. He led Jamil under an arcade, where they waited for the shipping agency to open. Someone walking past in a hurry waved them away and said something Mokdad did not understand, but the doctor and the child did not move. It was some time before the doctor saw the man opening the agency, which was the only place that sold tickets. The man behind the desk was surprised to see customers.

'We want tickets for the ferry,' Mokdad said in English.

The man stared up from his desk. 'You the foreigners staying at the circus?'

'What time is the ferry due? We need two tickets.'

'I've heard about you. Why did you come here?'

'We lost our way,' Mokdad said. 'How much are two tickets? Does the child have to pay?'

'Full price. Concessions are only for citizens of this country.'

'Give us two.'

The man's eyes moved from the doctor to Jamil, then to the money in the doctor's hands. Still in silence, he swivelled round in his chair to switch on an old computer behind him. The rain stopped tapping on the windows and moved out to sea. The only sound was the noise of the old computer.

'What are your names?'

The foreign names baffled the agent despite having them repeated to him several times. In the end Mokdad wrote them on one of the yellowed sheets of paper that littered the desk.

'Give us the cheapest tickets,' he said. 'I suppose the ferry will be coming quite soon?'

'In two hours,' the shipping agent said. 'That's when it's expected.'

'Does it leave straight away?'

'Why should it wait?' With his head moving back and forth between the paper and the keyboard, the agent punched the names in with a single hesitant finger. He asked with his back to his customers, 'What happened to the others you were travelling with?'

'I don't know.'

The man turned round with a sardonic smile. 'Every man for himself, eh?' He printed the tickets and asked for the money. 'You're guests in this country,' he said. 'Don't overstay your welcome.'

He turned back and hit a button on the keyboard. Somewhere out of sight an old printer began to drone. When it turned silent again, the agent bent down and emerged, breathing heavily, with their tickets. He asked for the money. The doctor watched him count it.

'Was it worth it,' the man said, 'making that journey? You risked killing your son and what for? If I were in your place... In war you have to take sides.' He put the money in his desk drawer. 'What were you doing there, eh? Were you in the army? You a deserter?'

'A doctor.'

'You were a doctor? What about all those dying?' the agent said. 'Who's going to help them?' He sat back in his chair and said, 'You almost got your son killed. I don't understand you people. If it were my country... Be a man. Don't run away.'

Three hours passed without any sign of the ferry, and they returned to the shipping agent's to ask if there was any news. The man behind the desk was not surprised to see them. 'Is the ferry coming?' Mokdad asked.

'Didn't anyone tell you?' The man shook his head with contempt. 'Forget the ferry. Not today. Cancelled because of the weather.' He raised his arms in the air and grinned at the ceiling. 'An act of God.'

'When did you hear?'

'Oh, an hour ago,' the shipping agent said. 'It never left the mainland last night. They don't bother to let us know. I had to call them myself.'

'When is it coming next?'

'No idea. A week, a month? I don't want to raise your hopes. We're a very unimportant port of call. If the weather happens to be bad again on that day, it might again not come.'

'And our tickets?' the doctor asked.

'No reason to worry,' the other said. He took out a handkerchief from his pocket, spat in it, folded it and wiped his nose, too. 'Your tickets will be valid even if it comes in a year's time. Ask your friend at the circus to put you up until it does.'

On the road back to the camp it started to rain again. Walking next to the doctor under the borrowed umbrella, Jamil was silent. Mokdad knew that the child was disappointed, that he had wanted to leave, but he himself was in a good mood, thinking about his return to the camp. He would have to be careful not to show how pleased he was when he explained to his host what had happened. He ought to apologise even though it was through no fault of his own; he ought to make sure that he spoke with plausible dismay and perhaps offer to help in the circus in return for being allowed to stay until the ship came in. 'Yes, I am afraid,' he would say, 'the ferry didn't come because of the bad weather. It is very disappointing. I apologise for burdening you, but I hope it won't be for more than another week. I have bought the tickets.'

Now he would have the chance to get to know the circus owner's wife and let her know him, too. He did not want her to remember him as a man without a home, without vocation, who took from them but had nothing to give back. He might tell her how he came to be there—no, that would be foolish; she would not understand. He felt Jamil's hand seeking his. He frowned while still looking straight ahead, his lips stretched into a grimace and he tried to move his hand away, but the child gripped on to it. He left his hand limp in the boy's clasp.

In the camp he went to return the umbrella. On the way he practised what he was going to say again, repeating the words in his mind until he knocked on the door of the caravan with an urgency that he hoped suggested enough concern but not alarm. There was no reply and he knocked again, to make sure there was no one in before going in search of the circus owner across the camp, and this time there was a slow shuffling of feet, the door opened and there stood the woman, staring at him. She had obviously been in bed. Her hair was jumbled, she wore a heavy gown, and her eyes, though sharply focused on him, were swollen from sleep. For the first time he had a clear view of her face, and, while he was engrossed in studying it, she wrapped the gown more tightly around herself and a pink patch on either cheek, which he could not decide whether to attribute to the cold or to bashfulness, tinted her pale skin. Mokdad greeted her appearance with the concerned expression that he had prepared for her husband, until her look of unease made him aware of the impression he was giving, and he opened his mouth to give the little speech he had prepared—about the cancelled ferry service, the storm, the regrettable prospect of staying on the island for another week or maybe a month. Then he hesitated. He did not want to make her think, not her, that he was sorry to be back. He had to say something else.

She spoke first, mumbling something in the low voice of someone who had just woken up. It sounded like, 'Doctor, it's you,' but he could not tell whether it was with surprise or in a mere matter-of-fact way. She did not repeat it, but he fancied that there was a shy joy in her little greeting and the possibility that she might be pleased to see him again made him want to say yes, it was him, he was back, he was glad not to have left. At the thought of making a fool of himself he held back at the last moment, and conscious that he had been holding her up at the door in the cold, he took a deep breath and said in a confessionary voice: 'Your husband was kind enough to lend me this umbrella.' Then he handed it over and, relieved, went off across the flooded camp, without looking back, his clothes already getting wet in the rain.

Seven

SINCE HIS RETURN from the port their caravan felt smaller.
It now only took Jamil a couple of steps to pace the room
from end to end; he could no longer move around without
bumping into the sole chair or the table, and his bed was
so narrow that he had trouble falling asleep. Everything
was dustier than he remembered it—and colder, too. As
soon as he woke in the mornings, shivering, he would
leave—escape, more precisely—before Mokdad woke up,

and would wander across the camp from the big tent to the animal enclosures. If it was not raining he would go for a walk in the fields.

But he still felt trapped. The island felt like a cage, a thought that was so potent sometimes that he could hardly breathe. When it seized him, at random moments during the day, an event triggered by the unprovoked suspicion that something might happen and he would be sent back to his homeland, he would run away from the camp, splashing through the mud, his trousers getting caught on the thorns, until he was exhausted. Then he would find the strength to tell himself that there was no reason to worry, that it would not be too long before they resumed their journey. Mokdad and he together: when he thought of him he ceased to be afraid. The doctor had saved his life and promised to protect him until they got to the place called Europe, and he spoke the foreign language and was very clever. Jamil had seen him treating the hurt elephant. He assumed he was an animal doctor without asking him because he knew that he did not like questions. He did not want to annoy him. On the way back from the town, after they had been told that the ferry was not coming, Jamil had been afraid that the man from the circus would not let them back in and they would have nowhere to sleep. He had taken the doctor by the hand. Men held hands at home, didn't they? It had calmed him down to feel they were joined together; it had somehow given him comfort to know that whatever was going to happen to him would happen to Mokdad, too. And the man had not pulled his hand away; he had not rejected him.

He wished that he knew how to show him his admiration. You could not call it…he shied away from the word *love*. Love was what his sisters always talked about, not men. And yet he blushed when he thought about it because he could not find a word that better described what he had felt when the man held him on the capsized dinghy that night at sea. They were *friends*, he decided, but the word fell short when he compared the man with the boys of his own age whom he had called friends. The answer, then, if he was to do justice to him, his true friend, was to dismiss his old friendships as insignificant, or, better still, as not friendships at all, merely as boys he had known from school or the neighbourhood and the mosque. Besides, he told himself, those boys were too far away now, he would never see them again. He did not miss them.

The first day of good weather he went back to the town. The sun was out, the clouds had scattered far out to sea, and the wind blew in furtive but very cold gusts. He walked with his hands in his pockets and half his head hidden in the zipped-up collar of a borrowed jacket. The streets in the town were almost empty; most shops were closed apart from a coffee shop filled with men whose voices, belligerent and incomprehensible, travelled out to the street through misted windows. Jamil wandered about observing everything with hungry eyes: the moored fishing boats, the yellow drift nets piled on the quay, the church bell tower, the statue of a bearded man in robes holding a crucifix in his outstretched arm. He did not recognise the Christian symbol; only the pigeons and the palm trees in the square comforted him with their familiarity and the memory of home. No, he did not want to think of home, he decided, resisting the effect it had on him, reminding himself that he never wanted to go back.

He could not read the signs but the advertising posters set his imagination alight: soap, soft drinks and milk chocolate, items that belonged to the kind of life he dreamed of, a life that had no forbiddances and never went short of anything. The image of his future in a big modern city living with Mokdad made him giddy with happiness. How many times had he dreamed of a life like that, which he had been convinced awaited him in adulthood? He did not have to wait any more; now he was free to live as he wished. On the waterfront he stared at the sea with an impatience that made his head throb. There was no need to worry: the ferry was due in two days, the sea was calm and there would be no more delay.

A shop along the esplanade selling cigarettes and sweets was open, too. In a wire cage placed close to the window to catch some daylight a green bird with a large bill squawked and flapped its wings. The smell of a burnt-out cigarette in an ashtray on the counter was still in the air. Next to the counter there was a rack with postcards, and a shelf with souvenirs displayed haphazardly. The cheap dusty trinkets caught Jamil's attention: they were more interesting than the exotic bird. He picked up a small ceramic donkey with a hat and panniers, and put it in his pocket just as a toilet flushed behind a door, which stood ajar at the far end of the shop: a man with broad shoulders and a bald patch was washing his hands with his back to him. Without turning round the man said something in an amiable voice, but when he came back into the shop, wiping his hands on his trousers, and saw the boy, his expression changed. He said something in the local language, frowning. Jamil pointed at a packet of chewing gum and gave the man a banknote. After he'd put a stick of gum in his mouth he held his hand out for the change, but the man waved him away testily.

Jamil walked out. Every injustice he suffered added to his dislike of the world. But he was nobody's fool: the little souvenir in his pocket, like everything he stole, was just retribution. He sat on a bench facing the sea, wrapped up in his jacket, and stared at the great expanse. He thought about his dead sisters, who had always been good to him. He wished they were alive. Was it a coincidence that the very moment he had lost them he had found Mokdad? He had never thought about God before. Going to the mosque had always been a nuisance, but he had never questioned God's existence. God belonged to the adult world, which was enough reason to regard Him with suspicion. Now, however, he had an idea that He looked after him, that He had sent Mokdad, the way He always sent His angels to people, to keep him alive and guide him through life.

It was consoling to believe that his sisters would be in paradise but he was uncertain about his mother, who would often punish him with a switch fashioned from a branch of the olive tree in their garden. He did not want to admit that he was relieved she was gone. She had done some good things, too, though... He remembered the presents on his birthdays and some given to him on random days, which made them even more pleasing. And he also remembered the occasions, only a handful, when she had regretted having punished him. All that he took into consideration as he deliberated, and then let God know that he forgave her and wished that she be sent to paradise too.

Satisfied with his magnanimity, Jamil sat back on the bench and gazed at the sea, chewing gum and swinging his legs. The sun was still bright but soon the wind picked up, the branches of the bay trees along the esplanade began to quiver, the fishing boats rocked, and white horses formed outside the harbour. A fear gripped him that another storm was brewing up out at sea and their departure would be postponed again. Growing despondent, he left the waterfront to return to the camp. Some distance from the town he took the small ceramic souvenir out of his pocket and hurled it at a wall on the side of the road. It smashed into colourful shards, giving him the satisfaction of having punished the man who had kept his change. He was startled by a voice calling him: he saw a man up the road. His heart beat fast; he had been caught. He wavered between staying or running away.

It was a respite from the storms that had ebbed and flowed for days, but according to the barometer it was only temporary. The rain would be starting again in a few hours, which Damianos did not want to spend working in the tent or on the phone to the banks. He found his shotgun, a pump-action Remington 870, and his cartridge

belt, put on his rubber boots, and let the circus hands know
that he would be back in the afternoon.

As soon as he was out of sight of the camp a deep
calmness came over him. The long walks in the country
were his only real pleasure these days. The hunting itself
was almost coincidental; after the girl's death he did not
enjoy shooting much. Taking a life seemed unnecessary,
almost wrong to him now, but he still raised the shotgun,
with a sinking feeling, and pulled the trigger, just to prove
to himself, he supposed, that he still had the strength not
simply to do it but to go on with what was left of his life.
It was as if he were telling himself that he was not afraid,
that the tragedy had not weakened him, and if death could
take a child so casually, if the world was indeed cold and
random, then he might as well join in the killing, without
remorse. The world could not get any darker.

There was good scrub on the hills on the other side
of the town, far from houses and farms, where he might
find some partridge this time of the year. He took the road
with the gun slung over his shoulder. Just the smell of the
sea and the feel of the cool air on his face were enough to
make him smile: like a famished man, he needed very little
to stay alive. Joy swelled up inside him, almost against his
will, and a little while later, unexpectedly, he felt a desire
to sing. Would that be absurd, an insult to his daughter's
memory? At first he could not bring himself to do it, but
there was no one around and shyly he began to hum an
old favourite tune as he walked. Was he really happy? he
wondered in disbelief. He had taken the road to town many
times before, mostly to call the banks in the capital from a

public phone out of earshot, but this was the first time he had felt that way. His hum grew louder the farther he got from the camp, and he matched his steps to the tempo of the music. He was walking fast, spurred on by his growing exhilaration, which he tried in vain to suppress. The road snaked ahead towards the sea and a bird of prey was suspended in the sky. He would not shoot it even if it were close. He paused with his thumbs hooked in his cartridge belt and watched it circling somewhere over the fields: it must have found some prey. He wondered whether it ever hunted for pleasure, as people did. Perhaps, why not? Who knew what an animal felt? He began to walk again, picking up the tune where he had left off. It was a sad song, but still it felt good to let go of a little emotion.

His humming was interrupted by what sounded like glass breaking. There was a child up ahead on the road. Damianos recognised the foreign boy who stayed in the camp. He raised his hand and called out a greeting, but there was no response from Jamil. When he came up to him, he grinned and spoke in his mother tongue even though he knew that the boy could not understand. 'Hello, hello. No reason to be afraid. It's only me. Don't you recognise me? I'm the boss.' And he chuckled. 'Out on a little walk?' Jamil stared at the shotgun. 'Walk. Walk,' Damianos repeated and demonstrated with his fingers. Again, Jamil did not react, and the man said, 'It's a nice day to be out, isn't it?' He looked up in the sky, exaggerating every remark and gesture like an actor on stage, to make himself understood. At last the boy nodded with reluctance. 'Are you all right?' the man asked. 'I think I heard…' He pointed at the scattered shards on the side of the road, but Jamil vigorously shook his head to deny—what? Damianos thought. He was not accusing him of anything. He waved his question away with a smile. 'Oh, it's not my business. Never mind. I'm going hunting,' he said and gestured what he meant. 'You want to come along?' He tapped the shotgun hanging at his side; he could tell the boy was fascinated by it. 'Come, come,' he repeated and resumed his walk. Jamil followed him reluctantly.

Damianos went on talking, without gesturing after a while, as though he had forgotten that Jamil could not understand him. He did not mind silence when he found himself alone or in the presence of his wife, whose taciturnity he accepted as one of the least painful wounds of their tragedy, but in any other company he could not stand it. He felt the urge to fill the silence with the sound of his own voice, could not help himself but say something, anything he could think of, no matter how trivial, and was not the least discouraged if his remarks did not induce his companion to join in. He would simply speak more and answer his own questions, and some said—his wife, incredibly, was not one of them—that he was making a fool of himself.

'I guess you can't wait to leave the island,' he said, walking ahead. 'Don't worry. Sooner or later the weather change and you'll be on your way.'

On a high point on the road he stopped and exclaimed, spreading his arms, 'Look at that view!' Jamil looked around indifferently, while the man nodded to himself with admiration. From that distance everything seemed perfectly arranged, like a painting composed according to some principle—the rule of thirds or the law of the golden section. But there was something perversely comforting about the unpeopled primordial landscape, too: it would still be there in a thousand years; none of the daily human horrors mattered. He felt moved. What was the matter with him today? He hitched up his shotgun and they set off again.

'The doctor told me what happened,' he said. 'Don't worry. Your troubles are over.' Jamil shrugged his shoulders and Damianos, convinced the boy had understood, beamed at him. 'Do you like the circus?' he asked. 'What do you like best? The animals or the acrobats? I've seen you in the tent, watching the acrobats. You'd have loved our show. But we don't give any more performances. There's no point. Everyone on the island has been to see the show. We weren't meant to still be here, you see, but we can't leave.' He continued, understood only by himself, 'It's because the banks would take the business away from me if I return to the mainland. Do you understand? Take everything away. Pounce on it like a tiger,' and he demonstrated. Jamil chuckled. 'We're trapped here,' Damianos continued. 'If I go, I'll lose the circus. Everything.'

He threw his hands up in the air and made the sound of an explosion. Jamil's eyes lit up with sudden fascination. He was a good boy, Damianos thought, now that he had had the chance to get to know him a little. He seemed the same age as his daughter when she died, more or less. Was he ten, twelve? He was nothing like her, though, he looked rather rough. Once, after a good hunt, a couple of years before the girl died, he had come home with the dead birds hanging from his cartridge belt and she had burst into tears. He had laughed. Oh, he was very different back then. Olga had reproached him, and he had never brought the kill into the house again if Anna was in. He could not imagine this boy crying over a few dead birds.

'Has anyone ever taken you hunting before?' he asked. 'Your father?' He raised his hands in imitation of shooting a gun. 'Boom, boom?' Jamil shook his head with a shy smile. 'You haven't? Well, then, let's see if you like it today.'

Near the town they got off the road and headed across the fields with the man walking ahead, the sea on their right, the roofs of the town within sight and the bells of a grazing flock of sheep chiming somewhere. They were still far from their destination. 'Are you tired?' Damianos asked. 'I should have told you we were going a bit far; there's nothing to hunt around here. You can go back if you want to. Just turn round and walk straight until you hit the road. Do you want to leave? I don't mind.' Jamil gave him his usual puzzled look. 'Leave,' the man repeated. 'Do you understand?' He raised his voice and again resorted to his improvised sign language. 'Leave, leave!'

Jamil's lips tightened in a hard pout and Damianos stopped. 'No, no, I'm not sending you away. I was only asking if you wanted to go. It's a little far where we're going. Far. Right? You can stay if you wish,' he said. 'Why don't you stay. Yes, stay.' Jamil watched the man's moving hands and nodded. 'Good,' Damianos said. 'Let's carry on, then.'

At a place where the scrub was dense he unslung the shotgun, loaded it, and gestured for the boy to stay behind him and be quiet. He then walked on softly, with the gun aimed at the ground, not talking any more. It would have been much easier to hunt with a dog, but he had never been interested enough in hunting to own one. Every minute or so he stopped, mounted his shotgun and waited in silence for a bird to flush, then after a moment started again. This was the part he enjoyed most, when his brain cleared of every thought and his senses converged on his task.

There was a flutter and a partridge flew out of a thicket somewhere out of view. By the time he turned in its direction and raised the shotgun, the bird was already far. He shot anyway and missed—to his relief, he felt. He stopped to replace the spent cartridge and smiled at the child. Jamil started saying something and now it was the man's turn not to understand. After a lot of gesturing he nodded. 'You want to have a go at the gun?' He chuckled. 'No, no, you're too young, little friend. You can hardly lift it.' The boy kept asking in his obscure language and waving his hands, but Damianos shook his head and started walking again. The next time he stopped to wait for any birds to flush he did not hear the boy behind him. He turned around and saw him already some distance away, walking back in the direction they had come from. He called at him several times but Jamil did not turn round or answer. Damianos vowed to speak to him later and went on deeper into the scrubland where the earth was rockier and the shrubs taller and denser, a small middle-aged man, his breathing laboured, alone in the wilderness, the wind becoming gustier as he climbed on to higher ground. After a while he paused again with the gun mounted and all at once felt a twitch of loneliness and a darkening of his mood. His mind was not on the hunt any more, but on having upset the child.

He heard rustling and he turned the muzzle of the shotgun towards the bush from which the sound had come just as a partridge flew out of it. The barrel of his gun followed its flight for a couple of seconds, then he fired and the bird dropped somewhere in the distance. He slung the gun over his shoulder and went to get his quarry. It had fallen into a tall thicket with thorny branches and no opening through it that he could immediately see. He had to walk around it, find another way in. Wet with perspiration, using the shotgun as a walking stick, his mouth twisted into a stubborn expression and his heart beating fast, he staggered as he circled the dense thicket. At some places the bushes slightly parted, but he could not fit through. If the boy had been there he might have helped him.

He had an idea that made him laugh: what if he asked the boy to stay with Olga and him? He was an orphan and they would treat him better than any institution, offer him a good life. Clearly the doctor was not interested in him. They might even adopt him legally. He had to tell his wife about bringing him up. But before telling her, he would ask Mokdad. His excitement at his idea, his hope that it would make Olga happy animated his tired body, and he resumed his search with great vigour, but when he tried to squeeze through the thorns in the thicket he scratched his cheek and it began to bleed. He abandoned the search for the bird and started back to the camp.

Far behind him Jamil had heard the shot as he went across the scrubland, stumbling over the thick grass, muttering to himself and kicking stones as he went. How foolish he was to expect anything from anyone; he had been treated badly so many times and been told he was too young for everything. But he had proved he was strong enough to survive and could take care of himself as well as any man. For a brief moment he had believed that the man from the circus was kind, that it had been nice of him to ask him along, but he had been wrong, wrong. What about the time he gave me money? he asked himself, but he dismissed that as unimportant. Money meant nothing to that man, Jamil told himself; he was very rich, he owned a whole circus. He had forgotten that he could not trust a grown-up; only the doctor would not let him down. He walked on, muttering to himself and kicking stones, scornful and miserable, contemplating the great unfairness of the world and how exciting it would have been to shoot the gun. The man had promised to let him shoot but changed his mind. Jamil wished that he had his catapult to show him how good he was, even though he could not have killed a bird as big as a partridge. He was really a great shot and he would have quickly learnt how to use the gun and he would have easily shot those birds—if only he had been given the chance.

Suddenly, he saw something on the ground and picked it up. A seashell fused into a stone. He had never seen a fossil before and he studied it with awe, wondering how it had come to be so far from the sea. He remembered his religious instruction about prophet Noah and the Great Flood when the sea had covered the whole world. It had to be the only explanation. He rubbed the dirt off it and ran his fingers over the intricate shape, then put it in his pocket and walked on, his mind returning to the circus owner and the hunt. He needed to speak to the doctor, his only friend, who understood him. He had to tell him how he had been humiliated by the foreigner. Oh, when would they leave this place? His eyes filled with tears. He was glad that the man could not see him crying now.

Eight

FROM THE MOMENT that she opened the gate and entered the enclosure carrying the bucket and broom, Shanti watched her silently, standing next to the tree where the other end of the chain around her leg was attached. That morning, for the first time, it struck Olga that, ever since the incident, the animal had never come up to her or flapped her ears or let out the little rumble with which she used to greet her. It made the woman feel ill at ease and unwelcome. At least, as far as she could tell when she inspected it, the wound was healing well, if slowly, and she spent a long time clearing the pus with peroxide and a gentle persistence, as though she wished to erase the wound itself away. But it was still there when she finished, in the animal's brown, wrinkled skin, a long, deep cut stitched with fishing line, which had snapped at a couple of places, revealing a few inches of red flesh. It would heal, even though it would take much longer than the superficial wounds in the elephant's neck where Olga's sharp broken stick had struck, but she knew that the memory of both would remain in the animal's mind as indelibly as the scars they would leave in her skin.

Once she finished caring for the wound, she dipped the broom in the bucket and began to wash Shanti with tentative movements. Unsure whether the animal welcomed her attentions, she paused to remove the padlock and thin chain. Shanti was free to go but did not move, and Olga resumed her task less uneasily.

At the far end of the camp Mokdad came out of the old caravan and made his way towards her in a cautious walk, which took him across the dry spots in the muddy ground. Watching him, she admitted that she was glad he had not gone, even if it were only for a few more days, even if it were only out of vanity: she had noticed his interest in her. She waved and he returned her greeting shyly. Everything about him was filtered through a natural reserve, which she assumed was made worse by the fact that he was in a foreign place, living on charity. When he came up to the enclosure, she smiled to make him feel welcome even though it had never been her natural reaction when she greeted someone. She wondered what other changes he would prompt in her.

'I cleaned the wound,' she said.

'Ah, good, good.' He crossed the gate and asked, making an effort to sound casual, 'How is our patient today?'

It was reassuring that he was not the cheerful kind either. It somehow made her feel that being happy to see him was not a betrayal of her grief: they were sad together. She finished washing Shanti and said, 'There is still pus in the wound.'

'Let me see.' He bent down to check the animal's leg, and immediately Shanti backed off, swinging her trunk from side to side. Olga spoke to her to calm her down and gave her a piece of fruit while Mokdad studied the wound. When he stood up again he said firmly, 'Don't worry. It looks reasonably fine.'

'What about the snapped stitches?'

'She hasn't been very careful, has she? It'll take a little longer to heal, that's all.'

A moment of silence lingered on while neither of them spoke. To stop it expanding into something awkward and fragile, Olga said without much thinking, 'I'm glad you didn't go. Can I say that? I hope you don't mind. You probably can't wait to leave this place.' But he did not reply, letting her find her way out of the maze that she had put herself in. 'It's only that it's good for Shanti that you're around,' she ultimately said. 'If her wound got infected I wouldn't know what to do.'

'You don't have to worry. Just keep it clean. Are you sure there isn't a vet on the island?'

'There isn't much use for one. There are only sheep, goats, a few stray dogs—and our animals these days, of course. Why? Do you mind looking after Shanti while you're still here?'

'Oh, no, not at all. That's not what I meant,' he said. 'Anything I can do to be of help, please let me know. I'm grateful to your husband and you for everything you've done.'

She regretted having trapped him with that question in order to escape from what she had said earlier.

'I'm taking Shanti for a walk,' she said. 'Would you like to come along? You haven't seen much of the island, have you?'

'No, I haven't been around the island. I spend most of the day in the caravan.'

'It's an awful place to stay.'

'Oh, I don't mind.'

'Why don't you come along, then? It's a nice easy walk to the sea. There are some trees Shanti likes the taste of down there. I think it's the salt on the leaves.'

He stood there perfectly still, looking at the animal, not replying. Olga wondered whether she had embarrassed him with her offer. After all, he was a foreigner, they were talking in a tongue that was neither's own, and hadn't he said that he wasn't a Christian? Muslims had a different sense of morality, for all she knew. His eyes avoided her and his lips were sealed while he deliberated whether to accept her invitation. Then he surprised her by pointing at

Shanti. 'What is that?' he asked. And, when Olga did not reply, he added, 'There. In her neck. Do you see?'

The woman looked at the crusted wound she had inflicted herself and feigned ignorance. She had lied to everyone who asked her what had happened that day in the hills, saying that the animal had fallen into a covered well while foraging in the scrubland. She knew without her husband telling her, which he had done anyway, that the elephant was their most valuable possession and if Shanti were ever badly hurt they would lose everything.

The doctor examined the animal's neck and said, 'Nothing to worry about. They aren't serious at all. They're healing already. Just let me clean them before we go.'

And that was how he agreed to join her on the walk. When she had first met him she had found his reticence comic, then had thought it was sad that, whether out of innate cautiousness or suspicion towards foreigners like her, he did not speak freely. But now, with the benefit of introspection, she could see that he was not much different from her, she who kept a large part of what she thought secret from everyone, her husband included, because they would not understand; or, worse, they would understand and somehow take advantage of her suffering. She did not know exactly what they might do, but she had unintentionally developed, she had to admit, a fear of intimacy, the way one contracted a chronic disease.

She gave the doctor the peroxide and the cotton wool, then stood by while he tended the neck wounds. When he finished, she walked Shanti out of the enclosure. Leaving the camp always improved her mood. In fact the farther she was from it, out of sight of the striped threadbare tent, out of earshot of the laughing circus hands, the training acrobats and snorting zebras, away from the animal smell, the better she felt. Her dark thoughts and memories started to lose their harshness and it was tempting to believe that, accordingly, there ought to be a place far enough from the circus where she might be happy again. But she had not managed to convince herself, not yet at least, that such a place existed.

After a spell of good weather, the days had turned cold and dark again, but now it only rained lightly and intermittently. That morning's rain, which had fallen while Olga was still in bed, had not been enough to flood the camp. All that remained of it were the glistening drops caught in the leaves of the bushes, which the animal brushed with her trunk as she went, collecting a few drops of water to wet her mouth. In the narrow path Shanti was careful not to touch the bushes with her injured leg, which Olga assumed still hurt. To help her, the woman walked next to her, guiding her around obstacles with gentle taps of the stick with blunt ends. At a place where the path opened up, the three of them walked alongside one another and Olga had the chance to be contrite about her earlier remark. 'I didn't mean what I said. I'm truly sorry you missed your boat. It must have been very disappointing. I hope this week…'

The doctor said, 'There won't be a boat for at least another month. I've asked the agent. The ferry broke down. The service has been suspended.'

'Oh, I didn't know that. I'm very sorry.'

'I've already told your husband.'

'You have? He hasn't told me.'

The sea came into view far in the distance, but the beach where Olga was taking the elephant was farther away, at the bottom of a bay fenced in with tamarisks, still out of sight. Only now did she realise, perhaps because she had not done it in human company before, that it was a very long walk, and she wavered in her certainty over whether spending the whole morning with the doctor would be agreeable. At least she got the impression that he was becoming more talkative, and indeed, not before long, it was he who broke the silence this time. 'I'm glad you don't want to be rid of the boy and me,' he said. 'You may rest assured we aren't trying to take advantage of it. I just wish we could afford not to rely on your hospitality.'

'Why? Are you too proud?'

'No, no,' he denied with a blush, failing to spot her humorous intent. 'I was thinking of your husband and you. The inconvenience. I can't pay for a room in the town. I have nothing. I lost everything at sea.'

'We like having you here, doctor,' Olga said, hoping to put the matter to rest.

He became taciturn again as they walked down the gentle slope towards the sea. She asked tentatively, 'Do you mind telling me your name again?' She had an idea that perhaps he was on the run and might want to keep it secret.

'Mokdad.'

'Is that your first name?'

'No. It's Qasim.'

Telling him hers felt like letting him in on a secret. She doubted that he would ever call her by it, but didn't want him to think of her just as the woman with the elephant or the circus owner's wife. She hoped that this face-to-face exchange of names would establish a little familiarity with each other, but what he said next, spoken with more than his usual earnestness, as though it had been in his mind for a long time before their cautious friendship allowed him to say it, still surprised her.

'You don't seem happy,' he said. 'Don't you like it here?'

It was the first time he had asked a question that did not concern him directly, and he kept his eyes fixed on the distance while waiting for the answer. She made no attempt to satisfy his curiosity. Receiving no immediate answer, he added an extra measure of politeness without withdrawing his question, 'Do you mind me asking?'

'I don't particularly like it anywhere, doctor. In fact this place is better than most.'

'I suppose I don't have the right to ask. But I couldn't help it.'

'Because you're a doctor?'

He chuckled. 'You may be right. We are used to be always looking for the underlying cause. Or maybe I'm just being indiscreet.'

'What do you think the *underlying cause* of my condition is? In your professional opinion?'

'I don't know you well enough to tell. I assume it has something to do with the island?'

She was briefly silent, then said, gazing into the distance, 'Do you mind the long walk? It seems much farther than I remembered it.'

He understood that he had overstepped the mark. 'I don't mind,' he said. 'I have nothing to do.'

He said no more and she let the silence stand between them, rejecting that way her own earlier attempt at familiarity. She normally took pleasure in the landscape and Shanti's company, but after a few minutes neither the wild bushes nor the ragged coastline nor the elephant, who ignored her gentle pats, had as good an effect on her as her conversation with the doctor, and she hoped that he would speak again. When he did, in what felt like a long time later, it was as though they had not stopped talking to each other. 'In fact,' he said, 'there was something I'd been meaning to ask you.'

She could not resist the temptation to say, 'Another diagnostic question?'

'No, no,' he said with a nervous chuckle again. 'I've been thinking I ought to be of some use while I'm here.'

'You've done a lot already. You are helping me with Shanti.'

'Perhaps I could help you more with her.'

'In what way?'

'Looking after her. Giving her morning wash perhaps? I could be taking her for her walks. Can you teach me how to guide her? Is it easy to learn?'

'I suppose it is. Shanti is very placid. She knows what to do in most cases herself. Do you really want to?' she asked.

'Yes, yes.'

'Elephants are emotional animals. She knows what you're doing for her. I have to warn you, though: you need to be patient. Be prepared to spend a lot of time with her, because she won't obey you unless she knows you well. I don't think you'll be on the island long enough for that,' Olga said, 'but if you still want to learn the basics, just to give you something to do while you are here, I'll be glad to show you.'

She handed him the stick and spent the rest of their walk to the sea teaching him how to guide the animal with his voice, gestures, and little treats that Olga carried in her pockets. Only when those failed did she allow him to use the stick to touch, with gentle pressure, the elephant on the places that she showed him, to make her obey. She cautioned him against hurting Shanti. 'Promise me,' she said, 'that you'll never treat her badly. And let me know immediately if she refuses to obey you.' She thought that the animal was fond of Mokdad, and she supposed that he might need less training than she had originally thought. Then she lagged a few steps behind, out of Shanti's field of vision, and let him guide her for a while alone. The animal did not seek her out.

It was afternoon now, the sun was still concealed by the clouds, but it was not as cold and windy as earlier on. They had almost reached their destination: she could see the trees concealing the beach. The path petered out and they had to walk among the bushes. The elephant knew the way; the doctor walked alongside her and Olga followed behind. There was no conversation; neither had spoken since she had finished explaining to him how to guide Shanti. The doctor was giving the animal all his attention now and Olga missed not having a conversation with him. She wondered whether she had been brusque. He had surprised her with his question. She had not minded him asking if she was happy, but how could she have answered? She was unsure how he had taken her changing the subject. Had he lost interest in her? She had been content with herself and her mourning, then had made the mistake of letting him in, innocently she believed, just to share a walk, and now, after a couple of hours together, it was not possible to dismiss him without suffering a little defeat, a return of the loneliness to which she'd thought she had become immune by virtue of her solitariness. She was still easy to hurt, like everyone, an open wound. She could have avoided it if she had not asked him along.

She decided to keep her distance, and slowed her pace while Mokdad and the elephant walked briskly on. It calmed her to turn her attention to the hills in the distance, the hazy sea, the cold touch of the wind against her face and the smell of the wild herbs her trousers brushed against. But soon those impressions left her and she felt alone and her mind turned to her husband, an unwelcome guest in her thoughts. That morning she remembered him, for no reason, as he had been at their daughter's funeral, standing at the open coffin (her colourless face was constantly on Olga's mind, all those happy photographs from before no longer registered), and remembered, too, how when the priest began the mass her husband had walked out. From that day on she had felt that she had been left to carry all the weight of her grief alone, but loathing him for it had eased her pain, had helped her live through the worst of her despair. Now, at last, she was starting to feel at peace with herself.

She observed Mokdad walking ahead, taking his task of guiding the animal very seriously. She wished that he would speak to her, say something, even if it was to ask her again why she was unhappy. She would answer him this time, tell him the truth. Maybe he had lost family over there in his country and knew what grief felt like. After waiting a few minutes for him to turn around she thought that she ought to speak up herself. If he had had the audacity to ask her a personal question, why should not she ask him if he had a family? Her trousers caught on a thorny bush and she fell further behind while trying to free herself. When she looked up again, Mokdad and the animal were coming to a place just before the beach where Olga knew the ground sloped a little steeply. Shanti's bell jingled, a sign that she was walking rather fast to get to the trees, and the woman called out to her to slow down, afraid she might have another accident, but the elephant took no heed of her. It took Olga aback; Shanti had never ignored her before. She called again but Shanti still went on and the woman caught up with Mokdad and asked for the stick back. Then she hurried ahead and tapped the front of Shanti's foot a couple of times. This time the animal slowed down, but made her displeasure known with a shake of the head.

Shanti walked down the short slope carefully, obeying the woman's verbal commands without the need for the stick again. At the bottom Olga gave her a piece of fruit and a pat on the shoulder. She led Shanti to the beach and let her go to the trees to eat. As soon as the doctor and she were alone she felt shy, another feeling that she thought herself not capable of at her age, and she said, trying to draw attention away from it, 'How do you like it here, doctor?'

'It is very nice. A beautiful place,' Mokdad said dutifully.

It was very quiet apart from the sound of Shanti snapping off branches and crushing them in her mouth. They were a long way from the camp; a few gulls bobbed up and down out in the bay and the surf broke on banks of seaweed along the sandy beach. The beauty of the place eased Olga's loneliness and, calmer now, not feeling shy any more, she had no qualms about asking the doctor whether he had a family. He answered without hesitation with a simple no, firm but not impolite, which convinced her that he was telling the truth. It pleased her to know that if he did like her, which she was almost certain he did, then she was the sole object of his affections. She took off her boots and invited him to do the same with his shoes, but he looked around indecisively as though she had asked him to undress. She explained to him that it would be unwise to keep them on if he wanted to walk with her along the beach. He balanced on one foot and with a child's modesty removed one shoe and peeled off the sock, then swapped feet and did the same with the other shoe.

The sand was cold but felt good against the hard soles of her feet. She looked at them as she walked and wondered if one could call them pretty. She had not thought about it before, as far as she remembered—had not pondered the aesthetic value of her feet according to the Western canon. Let me see now, she told herself. The ball was not prominent, the bridge curved smoothly, the toes were straight, she had no bunions…what's not to like? The ludicrousness of it made her laugh and she could not stop. Mokdad looked at her and smiled apprehensively, perhaps fearing that she was mocking him. Olga checked herself and apologised, embarrassed by her reaction. What was the matter with her? That change in her lately—the burden of her mourning lifting, her sudden exuberance—she could not tell the exact time it had come about. It felt almost like the days before her daughter's death—almost, because what had happened to her still gave her a nagging guilt. Olga did not know whether the lifting of her spirits would last or if it was only a brief respite from the pain, but she did not want to fight it down.

She wondered what the foreign man would make of her, laughing like that. His trousers neatly rolled up to the ankle, keeping a respectful distance as he walked alongside her, he did not seem that different from people that she knew. When she thought of the East, *One Thousand and One Nights* came to mind, women wearing the hijab, a minaret and the whirling dervishes, but he did not belong to that imagery. He was just like everyone else; his foreignness cast a faint shadow over him, but he was conscious of it like an ugly scar, which he tried to conceal.

She couldn't think what to say to him. They were coming to the end of the beach, but they had not said anything to each other since she had laughed unexpectedly. Shanti would be feeding for a while, and Olga had to find a way to pass the time somehow. She had a desire to get to know the man who helped her with the animal, to ask him about his country and listen to what he said in his heavy accent and calm manner. She decided to say something as soon as they reached a mossy rock in the sand, ask him about medicine perhaps, some friendly, inoffensive question that he would not refuse to answer; but they walked past it without saying anything. She promised to do it when they came to the end of the beach but then had a better idea. She asked him to put his shoes on and follow her.

She led the way over the rocks at the side of the bay to a large beach beyond, where the rusted hulk of a ship lay half-buried in the shingle. She only wanted the doctor to see it but he was eager to get to it, and she followed him, amused by his childlike fascination for the old freighter, which had run aground on the island many years before and now stood still as a rock, tilted to one side, the seawater and wind having long stripped it of most of its paint. He insisted that they climb on to it, which she thought unsafe, but she relented without much resistance, secretly welcoming his unexpected and unguarded exuberance. At a place where the hull was buried deep in the ground they stepped on to the deck with an easy climb and wandered around the dead ship, up and down ladders, in and out of rooms, all the way to the bridge, from which they could see far behind the shingle beach, across the rolling scrubland where there were no signs of human presence, no grazing animals, no pens or houses. Olga's pleasing sense of solitude returned and she admonished herself for her earlier dark mood. She was at ease with the foreigner, did not feel that she had to say anything, did not wonder what he thought of her.

While they stood there gazing at the hills in the distance and the sea in the opposite direction, with the wind whistling through the dark passageways and the glassless portholes of the hulk, and their shoes clanging against the steel floor, Olga became aware of a feeling of intimacy creeping up on her. It made her uneasy and she said that they should go. She led the way, down the rusty ladder to the deck and along a passage back to the place where they had climbed up, but before jumping off the ship she heard a cry and turned to see Mokdad holding his head. He had hit it against an overhanging bar.

'Are you all right?' she asked.

'Yes, yes. I was careless.'

She helped him climb down from the ship. 'Come and sit down,' she said, 'let me have a look at it. Does it hurt?'

'It's nothing,' he said.

'I can see it starting to swell up.'

'Sorry for the trouble,' he said.

'Shall we go back to the camp so that you can put something on it?'

'Let's stay here a little longer.'

She sat down next to him and said, 'It's my fault for bringing you here. It wasn't safe climbing on it.'

'It's been a nice change. I'd be doing nothing in the camp.'

'I don't have much to do myself.'

'You are at home,' he said as though it ought to be enough.

'If you can call a caravan home.'

'You aren't in a hurry to get back to the camp, are you?'

'No, no. Shanti takes her time with her food.'

'I know I'm not very good company,' he said.

'I'm glad you came along.'

He nodded in a way that suggested he was merely acquiescing. After a moment he said, 'Would you believe it? I haven't stopped thinking of home.' His sudden frankness surprised her: he sounded like someone else. 'And what happened at sea,' he added.

'It must've been terrible.'

He hesitated, then dismissed the temptation to tell her. 'Nothing, nothing.'

'You miss your home.'

'I don't know if I did the right thing after all.'

'Leaving, you mean?'

'I was afraid.' He looked at her searchingly. There was nothing suggestive about it; it felt as if he needed to know whether he could trust her. 'I haven't told anyone. You aren't from there, I don't mind telling you. I couldn't stand it any more. All I could think of was being killed. Shot at, or buried in rubble alive.'

'You did the right thing.'

'No, I'm a doctor. I am supposed to be helping people.'

'You can be a doctor anywhere, can't you?'

'I was needed more over there. There weren't enough of us. But I didn't even let them know I was leaving. I couldn't bear it. I just left.'

'You wouldn't be of any use dead,' she said. 'You could go back one day.'

'I'll have to live with the shame for the rest of my life.'

'You still have the chance to do good. You did help the boy at sea, didn't you?' She did not know that he had really saved Jamil's life. She added, 'And now you look after him.'

'No. I only promised to stay with him until the end of the journey. I can't help him after that. There will be people to help him where we're going, won't there? I wouldn't know what to do with him. I'm not good with children.'

She did not know why she said, 'I had a child, too. A girl—' maybe to match his openness.

'I see.'

'Does that answer your question? Why I'm unhappy? Is it so easy to notice?'

'If you care to pay attention.'

She had not talked to anyone like that in a long time. She said, 'Do you care? You've only been here a few days.'

He said, irrelevantly she thought, 'I wish I weren't afraid. I'd seen many people die in the hospital, but it's different in a war. No dignity—just ugliness... What happened to your daughter?'

She did not want to talk about the girl after all.

He said, 'I wish I knew you better.'

'There's not much worth knowing.'

'I think we should be getting back.'

It was her turn to say, 'We can stay a little longer. If you want.'

'Yes.'

They sat facing the sea next to the wreck and seemed to have agreed not to talk for a moment. The sky was heavy with clouds and the surf broke quietly on the shingles. She checked the swelling on his forehead and when she touched it, very carefully, he shut his eyes and made a little moan and raised his hand instinctively, just to move hers away. He held it in his, looked down and said, 'You're being kind to me,' before letting her hand go and lying on his back with his arm over his eyes. Again neither said anything and she lay down too, next to him, without their bodies touching. His breathing gave her the impression of a ticking clock. She only had to tell him it was time to go and he would obey, but instead, after a moment, she turned towards him and put her arm around him. His body quickly aroused her. When they made love she felt neither unease nor passion, but the calm conviction that she was setting herself free from grief. Lying back afterwards, she was quiet and thoughtful.

'Was it wrong,' he asked, 'what happened?'

'No, no. I wanted to. It's a long time since I felt like that.'

'I have no right to ask for anything,' he said. 'I'm only your guest. Tell me what to do.'

She felt a sudden sense of aversion towards talking. She would rather be alone. Now it felt as if they had been there a long while; they ought to go. Shanti would be looking for them.

'Oh, you don't have to do anything,' she said. 'Don't be so polite.'

He stood up and brushed down his clothes, and they walked back in the direction of the other beach, where they had left the elephant.

The doctor said, 'You can trust me.'

'I know. I'm not worried. I'm happy.'

'I'll do whatever you want me to,' he said, and she wished that he would stop talking. Shanti was eating beach grass, but followed her without complaint when she called her. They took the path back to the camp, Olga walking briskly ahead, a little in a hurry, expecting her contentment to drain at any moment.

Nine

IT TOOK JAMIL a long time to find the right piece of wood, going quite far from the camp and stopping at each tree that he came across in search of the right wood in terms of strength and shape. He settled for a branch of locust, which he could only snap off by swinging from it. Back in the camp he mimed to give the circus hands to understand that he needed to borrow some tools, and spent the rest of the morning fashioning the catapult. When he finished he inspected his creation and declared himself satisfied, certain from experience that it was the best he had ever made. But he had to try it out to know that it worked as well as it should. He returned to the field behind the camp and walked deep into the shrub to find a target, picking and discarding stones as he went, filling his pockets with large round ones, which would be the most accurate to shoot. The seashell fossil was in his pocket too, and he took it out and put it in another pocket by itself. Since he had found it, it had become a talisman to him. It was obviously something rare and he had the vague notion that it ought to be valuable, a sign of good luck. Every morning he took it out and rubbed it to clean off the smallest specks of dirt, then studied its whorls and ribs and tried to imagine what forces of the universe had put it in his path and made him find it.

After a long walk he came to a clump of trees, loaded the catapult and watched his step so as not to make much noise. He listened to the chirping and searched the foliage with his eyes until he spotted a bird and took aim. He had done this many times: shooting birds was one of the few fond memories of home. He felt calm and confident, but his stone struck the branch a few inches away from the target and the bird flew away. He adjusted the rubber band and chose a rounder stone to try again, but now the birds had turned silent and he could not make them out among the branches and leaves. Waiting, listening to the sound of his breath, he felt lonely. That sense of isolation was a recent sensation. He did not know how to deal with it, had never felt it before coming to the island. There had always been people around at home—family, friends and acquaintances, even when he did not want company. And there was the local language, too: he did not understand a word of it, it made him suspicious just to hear people speak. Only the doctor could ease those ugly feelings, but the man spent little time with him outside their caravan. Earlier that day Jamil had looked for him in the camp, wanting to show him his catapult, but could not find him anywhere. If his sisters were alive he would have company now.

He circled the trees quietly, holding the loaded catapult, and kept searching. He tried to imagine how impressed the doctor would be if he showed him a bird that he had killed. He bet he would pat him on the shoulder and laugh and say well done, because everyone knew it took great skill to hunt with a catapult. Jamil craned his neck searching for a target, the desire burning inside him to prove to everyone, no matter what his father and teachers used to say, that he was not a little boy but a man capable of great things. Then he heard it, a birdsong starting with a *seep seep seep* and followed by other familiar phrases: *filip filip filip, tereret tereret...* He recognised the sounds from home with spontaneous nostalgia while trying to trace the sound. The thrush was standing on a branch near the top of the tree closest to him. He raised the catapult, stretched the rubber band, took aim, and shot without hesitation. The stone ripped through the leaves and the bird fell, striking the branches on the way.

When he picked it up he saw that its cream black-spotted belly still moved up and down. He felt uneasy. He had hit birds that had not died before but never bothered with them, because his mother had forbidden him to bring them home, so he would abandon them alive where he had shot them. This time, however, he needed to show his trophy to the doctor, and he cradled the bird in his hand indecisively, running his fingers over the sticky blooded feathers, as fascinated as if he were studying a mechanical toy. He felt no pity for the small animal, which looked back at him glassy-eyed, and yet he hesitated. Looking nervously around and working himself up into a rage aimed at his reluctance to do what needed be done, he shut his eyes and finally, with a resolute move, wrung the bird's neck. A few little bones snapped inside the warm soft body and when he opened his hand again the bird lay limply in his bloodied palm. He had done it: he had taken a life with his own hands. A sense of awe made him shudder. Wasn't killing what men did with such ease? He was not that different from a grown man any more.

When the war had come to the city where he lived, he would go to watch it. Those had been small-arm fire-fights that had not lasted long. The fighters would run out of ammunition or get frustrated with not having a clear objective, and would withdraw to continue the fighting in another street, on another day. At first he stood some distance away, satisfied just to listen to the sound of gunfire, but before long its novelty had worn off and his curiosity pushed him closer to the line of fire, the barricaded streets, the burning cars, the houses pockmarked with bullets from where he watched the skirmishes, holding his breath a few feet behind the shooters. It had something of the excitement of a football match, until someone got hit. Horrified by the sight of blood and the cries of pain, Jamil had left the fighting and returned home, but could not stop thinking about it. It had taken several days for the horror to subside, but then he'd found himself trying *not* to forget the details of what he had witnessed. The wound, the bloodstained clothes, how the man had screamed: he kept turning it all over in his mind, not with revulsion but compulsion.

A week later he returned to the fighting. This time he followed even more closely behind the men, observing every detail with unblinking eyes until he heard that someone had got hurt. Then he would go to find him, worm his way through the other men to look at the injury, showing no emotion at the sight of the tangle of blood, flesh and bone—like a doctor, one might have said, but in truth with a fascination that Jamil knew not to confess to anyone, the way he never admitted his disappointment when a fire-fight happened to end without casualties.

The first dead man that he saw, after a month on the front line, was not what he expected. His eyes were slightly shut as though squinting into the sun, his lips were drawn to reveal clenched teeth, but there were no signs of violence on his body other than a trickle of blood, already dry, running from the edge of his mouth to the jugular notch. Nevertheless he was dead, of that there was no doubt, and Jamil had bent down to touch him so that he would remember for ever the day when he had first touched a dead man; but someone had pulled him back as he was stretching out his hand and slapped him in the face. He had returned home. Later the same man had come to the house and told his mother that he had seen the boy at the fighting, and she had beaten him and not let him leave the house alone again. The war had gone on, with many dying every day since, but he had seen no more of it.

He put the catapult in his pocket and turned in the direction of the camp with the dead bird in his hand. He had gone a short distance when he spotted the elephant far away and, after he had had a better look, the doctor walking alongside it, too. Immediately he went towards him, eager to show him the bird, but stopped when he saw the woman and instead followed them at a distance across the fields. He did not want to be near her. It annoyed him that every time she spoke to him she made him blush. He would try not to, but it would be impossible to stop his cheeks from burning while she asked him something in English, the other incomprehensible language, which the doctor could speak, too. All he could do was to look at his feet and wait with his hands in his pockets, listening or mumbling some answer, which the doctor translated before letting him go. It was something about the way she talked to him. He could not describe it easily: her keenness to know things about him; her hand touching him, which embarrassed him; and her pity, which he disliked. He had never liked women much, apart from his sisters. He had always felt ill at ease in their presence, did not like the smell of their perfumes, their headscarves, their habit of pinching his cheek. And of this woman he felt jealous, too, more than anything else, seeing her so close to his friend. He thought that he ought to ask Mokdad to come hunting with him tomorrow. He could teach him how to shoot the catapult if he wanted.

He guessed that they were headed for the sea. It was where the path led, not too far away. He followed them, walking far behind in the brush, keeping them in sight, careful not to be seen, telling himself that he would turn back before they got there, but he stayed with them until they came to the beach and watched them from behind the tamarisks, while the elephant fed and they stood on the edge of the water. When they walked to the far end of the bay and began to climb the rocks, Jamil set out to follow them again. For a while the trees concealed him from the couple, but he had to wait until they had gone over the rocks and disappeared from view before he could come out in the open and run after them. Except, by the time he reached the top of the rocks, the couple was nowhere to be seen. He scanned the shingle beach in every direction, at the foot of the rocks below him, the broom bushes with yellow flowers along the beach, but did not see them, and he decided that they must have walked to the shipwreck in the distance. He made a long diversion to get closer to it, hiding behind the bushes and large rocks on the way, and finally saw them standing on the ship's bridge. He watched from his hiding place, crouching, keeping still, breathing quietly, the dead bird always in his hand, while the woman helped Mokdad down from the wreck and sat next to him. They talked in low voices but he could still hear them, and, although he could not translate, he could sense, from the couple's closeness to each other, their intimacy.

At first, watching from his hiding place, he did not understand. Then he recognised with an uneasy feeling what was happening. Once a boy at school had passed him a creased magazine in the playground and he had had a quick glance, enough for what he saw in its pages to stay in his mind for months. He had never seen those acts in real life until now. It was not the way he had imagined it from the photographs. He was startled by what alternately sounded like moans of pain, grunts of rage and gasps for air, convincing him that the two people joined together were hurting each other. They reminded him of two animals locked in a death struggle until, at the height of their fight, they relented quite suddenly as though they had decided that neither could win, and lay back down wounded and both defeated.

What Jamil had watched had given him no thrill, only dread. It was a sin according to his religion, that much he knew. He did not know if the woman's Christian god forbade it too, but his friend had done something terrible and he felt great pity for him. His mind was swamped with images of horror: Maalik and his nineteen guards of Hellfire chaining the sinners whose skin oozed pus and beating them with iron scourges. It was the woman's fault. He had no doubt that she had tricked the doctor into it, and he praised himself for knowing all along not to trust her. He remembered once his mother telling a visitor at home how the day before, on her way back from an errand, when the shops were closed and there was no one in the streets, she had cut across the park and seen someone they both knew, a married woman, in the pine trees with a man who was not her husband. His mother had talked in a low voice and Jamil had pretended not to be paying attention, while her visitor had nodded gravely and taken another sweet from the plate in front of her. What would his mother have said if she had seen what he had today?

He moved backwards on his hands and knees, his head bowed, his body close to the ground, keeping behind the bush and trying not to make any noise, until he was far enough away to stand without being seen. There he stayed a moment, watching them leave the beach in the direction of the bay where the elephant was, then he turned and walked into the scrubland. They went out of sight but he knew that he would see them again in a few minutes when his route would bring him to the path that led back to the camp. He walked on alone in the dense growth of tamarisks, a young, troubled boy with closely cropped black hair, holding a dead bird. When he thought that they ought to be coming he paused and gazed at the path to the beach but they did not appear. He waited but time passed and he began to suspect, with a twinge in his stomach, that they were sinning again. After a while, with still no sign of them, he went back towards the beach to find out.

He was not far from the trees when all at once the elephant walked out, saw him and trumpeted. Jamil stood terrified, not knowing what to do. If you ran away from a dog you risked being chased; perhaps an elephant would react the same way. He doubted whether throwing stones at it would be the best way to chase it off. Nevertheless he picked up the largest stone he could find, determined to use it if he had to. The next moment Mokdad and Olga came out of the trees.

The woman beamed. 'Well, is that your young friend, doctor?'

Jamil dropped the stone and looked down: he had been caught. Mokdad said bluntly, 'What are you doing here?'

'Nothing.'

Olga said, 'Did Shanti scare you? I'm sorry, dear.' She turned to the doctor. 'Tell him not to be afraid.'

The doctor stared at Jamil with suspicion. He said in their language, 'How long have you been here?'

'I came from the camp.'

'When? Just now? Where were you? Tell the truth.'

'I was hunting in the fields behind the camp. I was looking for you... I wanted to show you. Look.'

He stretched his hands and offered the dead bird to the man, not daring to look him in the eye, and smiled timidly, waiting to be praised. Mokdad glanced at the bird and again frowned at him. Jamil said with wavering pride, 'I shot it,' and his heart jumped at the thought of the doctor catching him out. He felt the urge to admit he had been spying on the couple before they forced him to, but said nothing.

'Is that a bird he's holding, Qasim?' the woman asked.

The last word was the only one Jamil understood. He had not heard the doctor's first name before and thought jealously how the woman had known it before him. If Mokdad understood how much he loved him, how he was his only friend, how he would do anything for him because he had saved his life and was kind to him, he would not need her. He looked at him and said pitifully, 'I can show you,' and his heart beat with a love he had not felt before. He said, 'We can go hunting together. There are some trees halfway to the camp.'

'Is it hurt?' Olga asked. She had a closer look. 'Oh, it's dead. Poor thing. Did he find it just now? Does he want me to help him bury it?'

Mokdad said, 'Please, don't worry about him. He didn't... He's fine.' He told the boy, 'Throw that thing away.'

Jamil threw the dead bird into the bushes. It had left a bloodstain in his palm. He began to rub it but it was impossible to remove. Under the two adults' stare he could not stop himself from blushing. He wished the woman would go away, taking the elephant and her sin with her.

'Tell him it's getting late,' Olga said. 'He'd better come along. It's quite far to the camp.'

'You come with us,' Mokdad said.

Jamil obeyed meekly, still rubbing his palm, keeping his distance from the large animal, his happiness gone. He had expected the couple to be ashamed of what they had done; their composure infuriated him.

'Don't be afraid of Shanti,' the woman said.

He did not know what she was saying. He looked at Mokdad to translate, but he walked on, ignoring him. Perhaps she was telling him to leave, he thought, so that she could be alone with the man again. He waited for her to wave him away but instead she smiled. She said, 'Shanti was just surprised to see you. I'm sure she recognised you. Elephants are very clever, you know.'

It was clear now that she was not sending him off. When she asked, 'Do you want to ride on her?' Mokdad translated but Jamil refused, furiously shaking his head. She insisted: 'Come on, you'll like it up there. Shanti is very calm. She is used to children.'

'You can if you want to,' the doctor said.

The woman beckoned Jamil over. 'Come on. It's a long way back. You must be tired already. You'll like it.'

Jamil said stubbornly, 'I don't want to,' still afraid of the animal and suspicious of the woman's friendliness. He said, 'Tell her no. I'm not tired… If she wants to go ahead, we—'

Mokdad said, 'It's fine if you don't want to. Don't be afraid.'

'I'm not afraid.'

'He doesn't want to,' the doctor told Olga.

'Is he afraid? I feel sorry for the poor thing. He's always alone. If there were any children at the camp…' She thought of Anna, who would have been a few years older than the boy now, how she would have taken him under her wing. 'I wish there were something we could do to cheer him up. Try to convince him to let me put him on Shanti, Qasim. He'll like it.'

'Go on, don't be afraid,' the doctor said.

The elephant stared at them, flapping her ears and swaying her trunk. Jamil's face flushed with embarrassment again. He said furiously, 'I'm not afraid.'

'Then do it,' Mokdad said. 'Don't be ungrateful. These people have been very kind to us.'

Jamil said, 'Tell her only for a little while,' and the

doctor nodded at the woman. She ordered the elephant to bend her front leg and showed Jamil how to grab the animal's ear and place his foot on Shanti's bent knee, then helped him swing his other leg over the elephant. They set off with the boy sitting stiffly on the elephant's neck, staring at the ground far below his feet, feeling humiliated. The two adults had conspired to punish him. He was convinced that he knew why: they had guessed he had spied on them on the beach. He looked at the doctor but could not see his face, only his back as he walked ahead with his hands in his pockets. After a few minutes Jamil got used to the animal's slow sway and started to notice its deep breathing. An involuntary fondness for it sprang inside him but he stayed sullen-faced and did not ask to be let down, riding the elephant all the way to the camp.

Ten

A VOICE STARTLED him awake and he opened his eyes into a blinding morning light. 'Did I wake you, doctor?' the voice said. Mokdad blinked, his heart beating fast from the sudden intrusion into his sleep. 'Were you asleep?' the circus owner asked again, climbing into the caravan without waiting for a reply. 'I saw the boy leaving. He isn't coming back right away, is he?'

'I don't know,' the doctor said hoarsely and thought of the woman on the beach with the shipwreck. He sat up in bed and put his feet on the cold metal floor, trying to guess why the man was there.

The other said, 'I suppose I could come back later,' but pulled up the chair.

Mokdad remembered how he was supposed to go hunting with Jamil that morning. The hand that had tried to shake him awake some time earlier must have belonged to Jamil. He had dismissed it tetchily. He was glad the boy had not insisted. It would be ridiculous to be shooting a catapult at his age. 'No, no,' he said, clearing his throat, 'please stay,' and imagined the man ordering him to leave because of what had happened on the beach. Had Olga told him? Outside, the shredded flags on the roof of the circus tent flailed in the wind. He looked around for his shoes but could not see them anywhere.

'It's a chance for us to have a chat,' the circus owner said. 'Alone. That boy follows you around everywhere, doesn't he? You are pretty much like a father to him.'

'I am looking after him for the journey.'

'Of course, even if he were here now he wouldn't be able to understand us. But it's better just to be alone—you and me. Why don't you teach him some English?'

'We aren't going to England.'

'Ah, right. Northern Europe, didn't you say? But English is the world's common language. Shall I close the door?' And again he did not wait for an answer, but stood up and did what he had suggested. The silence gave an air of gravity to their meeting despite the other man's friendliness. Mokdad still looked for his shoes. They were under the bed and he put them on: wearing them made him feel less vulnerable. Beyond the shut windows and the door, the camp was coming alive with voices and animal calls and the noise of hammering.

'Looking after an orphan is a big responsibility,' his host said. 'You should be proud of yourself. You are an honourable man, doctor.' He sat on the edge of the chair and his eyes moved around the room, taking in the old furniture, the dirty floor and tattered curtains. He said with slight embarrassment, 'Are you comfortable here?'

The doctor did not want to sound ungrateful. He said, 'Yes, yes, thank you,' and his visitor seemed relieved to hear it, even though he knew it was untrue. It could not have been the reason for his visit, he was just casting around for something to say. Mokdad waited for him to speak again.

'How is Shanti?' Damianos asked.

'She is doing fine. It will take a while for the wound to heal properly.'

'Good. I haven't thanked you for your help. Shanti's been with us for a long time. My wife has grown very attached to her. An intelligent animal and very precious to the business, too. If anything happened to her I'd be ruined.' He said, 'I know her accident was my wife's fault. Olga can be very impulsive.' He gave the doctor a lingering look. 'But I can't blame her. She's been through a lot.' The hint of intimacy between them was cut abruptly by silence again, and both men stared out of the window to avoid having to look at each other.

It was the circus owner who restarted the conversation. 'You will be leaving soon,' he said. 'The weather will improve and the ferry will get fixed. I'm told it breaks down every year. Do you look forward to leaving?'

'We have already stayed too long. If it weren't for your hospitality we'd have slept in the streets.'

'No, no, please,' the other said with sincerity. 'My pleasure.'

The doctor thought of Olga. It was the time when she went to wash the elephant and treat her wound. He said, 'I wish there were something I could do for you, too.' It just felt the polite thing to say: the other man wanted something from him, but he had no clue what it might be.

'Tell me about the boy. What do you know about him?'

'I don't know him well. He doesn't talk much. Maybe it's my fault. I'm not good with children.'

'Does he have any family left? Back home?'

'I don't believe so. Either way, he doesn't want to go back. He's told me so.'

The other man beamed. 'Are you certain about that?'

'Yes.'

The next silence lasted less time before the circus owner said gravely, 'Mokdad—can I call you that? We had a child. Has Olga told you?' The doctor did not answer and his visitor continued. 'Yes, well, it's a private matter. Not the kind of thing one would tell a stranger. At any rate, our daughter was killed in an accident a few years back. We miss her terribly. She was our only child, no older than your little boy in fact. Jamil? Isn't that his name? I suppose you don't want to grow too attached to him. Do you plan to hand him over to social services when you reach your destination?'

Hearing it said like that made the doctor uncomfortable. To 'hand him over' sounded as if he would be abandoning Jamil, shirking his responsibility. He thought that perhaps the man was trying to shame him; he did not know to what purpose. He said, 'I would have to. What else could I do? The authorities…' disguising his detachment as law-abidingness.

'There is another solution. You could leave him here, doctor. Here, with us. My wife and I will care for him.'

'With you?'

'Yes. We know how to bring up a child.'

'Is that legal?'

The circus owner gave him a mocking look. 'Was your crossing the sea legal, doctor? I'm sure we'll find a way. We only wish to provide him with a happy life. What is wrong with that?' He leant forward and touched the foreigner on the knee. 'Please don't mention any of this to my wife,' he said in a lower voice. 'I haven't told her yet. I wanted to make certain the two of us could reach an understanding first.'

'Would she like to have the child?'

'Frankly, I don't think she'd agree if I just asked her. But if she gets the chance to know the boy better, spend time with him, she'd grow to like him. A child would help her, I'm pretty sure about that.'

'And what exactly do you want me to do?' the doctor asked. 'Talk to the boy?'

'No, no, heavens, no. Not now. I don't expect him to like my idea either. He's obviously very shy—and sus-picious, no? Oh, very suspicious of everyone apart from you. He clearly likes you and you can influence him, subtly of course, over a period of time.'

'There isn't much time left. You said so yourself.'

'Yes, that's what I wanted to talk to you about. Find an excuse to stay on. Let's say until summer? That would give Olga and me enough time to get to know him. And him to know us, too. What do you think?'

'I don't think he would like that. He can't wait to leave.'

'Find some excuse, my dear doctor. Lie to him if you have to. It'd be for a good cause. Don't you want him to have a good life? I can assure you my wife and I would take great care of him. You just said that you aren't good with children. What's stopping you from helping us?' He took a quick glance out of the window, an instinctive reaction to see if anyone was coming, and added ardently, 'Don't be in a hurry to move on from this place. You are in Europe now. You've made it, dear friend. Stay here a little more. You're safe. It'll only be for a few more months.'

Mokdad's expression did not change but a great relief, a reluctant joy took hold of him at the thought that again he was being prevented from leaving. The circus owner was still speaking, trying to convince him that he would not have to worry about anything if he agreed to stay. He was prepared to pay him enough to last him until he reached his destination. Damianos said, 'It'll be very hard to make it across Europe without money. What do you think?'

The doctor nodded in agreement, said nothing for a while, wanting to give the impression that he was struggling to decide. 'Very well,' he agreed, finally. 'I'll stay on the island for a few more months to see if I can convince the boy. But could we have somewhere better to stay?'

'Certainly. Leave it with me. I'll find a nicer caravan for you.'

He stood up and shook the doctor's hand, reassuring him that he would be doing an act of great kindness, when both knew that it would be nothing other than an act of betrayal.

Eleven

EVEN THOUGH IT was a cold Sunday, cold enough for the
worshippers to keep their coats buttoned up and their
hands in their pockets, reluctantly removing them to cross
themselves, the sun slanting through the stained-glass
windows tempted their eyes away from the ambo where
the priest was delivering a long homily on the theme
of repentance. It was a lecture that had edged towards
its climax several times already, only for the priest's

excitement to wane at the last moment, to everyone's disappointment, and for his voice to resume its tepid rambling tone. It had been meant to be a short sermon, but the priest had overestimated his oratory skills as much as his sense of humour. Earlier that morning at home the bathroom mirror had understood his every word, approved his turns of phrase, admired his profundity and laughed loudly at the witticism that he had risked inserting between his moral pronouncements; but later, as he had stood dressed in his heavy gold-threaded vestments in front of his congregation, his eloquence had deserted him a few sentences into his sermon like a coward brother-in-arms at the first sound of gunfire. His amusing anecdotes had failed to spark a single laugh, not even from the children. He had panicked, and his sentences had got lost in the labyrinth of his moral argument. When he thought that he could see some light at the end of a sentence he would hurry towards it but come to yet another dead end where he paused, coughed and stroked his beard while his eyes roved around the church pleadingly. Then his nouns would turn around, his ornate adjectives steel themselves, his verbs take a deep breath and his speech would plod on.

Damianos looked at his watch, then his eyes travelled to the domed ceiling where Christ Pantocrator stared down at him. Why had he bothered to come? the all-powerful judge of humanity asked him. The previous night Olga and he had slept as usual on opposite sides of the bed despite his attempt at touching her at one point, a suggestion that had been rejected with a faint but unambiguous grunt. In the morning, watching her getting dressed, he had noticed that her mannerisms, the intricacies of her behaviour, the way she laid her clothes out on the bed and the way she combed her hair or checked herself in the mirror—everything he remembered from the early days of their marriage—had changed. He was surprised that it could have happened without him noticing, as surprised as though he had discovered a scar on his body. And so, when she had climbed down from their caravan to go to church he'd felt compelled to follow her, driven by the urge to start getting to know her all over again and restore their old intimacy. He had told her to wait, had put on his Sunday suit, a shirt that was missing the collar button so he had used the red bow tie from his ringmaster's uniform instead and walked with her to town.

It had not worked. They had said nothing to each other on the way, he could think of nothing to say, saw nothing to give him an excuse to start a conversation, which would chip away at the wall built between them. He could tell that his company was unwelcome. There was no way he could speak to her about the boy yet. He regretted joining her, and hearing his daughter's name read out *in memoriam* by the priest during the service, a name that meant nothing to anyone apart from his wife and him, had upset him. It felt like a desecration of her memory to share it with an indifferent audience. No, not quite indifferent, he thought, and imagined the unfamiliar name arousing the curiosity of the locals, who must have guessed that it belonged to the couple from the circus who sat a few rows from the front. Damianos turned his eyes to the window and squinted at the glow of the morning light.

In a flash of memory the priest remembered what he had meant to say, and, confident at last, speaking clearly, his eyes hovering over his congregation, he was swept along by the flow of the words that had until then refused to obey him. Nothing was going to prevent him from finishing his homily now, he could recall every sentence to the end of his speech, and yet he slowed down, pronouncing every word carefully as if it were food that ought to be savoured. His audience sensed all this and fixed their eyes on him with something resembling awe for the first time that morning while he spread his arms and his voice rose to a crescendo. Sin, hell, fire and brimstone were all there at last in his sermon, the best one he had given in living memory, and he spoke on, he was unstoppable now...until the loud creak of the church door swinging on its hinges brought his voice crashing down to earth. He stopped, and everyone turned around. Emerging from his ecstasy, he would not have been surprised if God had walked in in all His power and glory, but instead there stood, framed against the glowing daylight, a stranger of below average height, with dark skin, a moustache, dressed in a windbreaker and dripping-wet trousers. He could not have been God, no, not by anyone's estimation.

Looking at the people who looked back at him, the man mumbled something in broken English, which was impossible to understand, and walked out, shutting the door softly behind him. His accent struck a familiar note with Damianos. After the priest had concluded his homily, offered Holy Communion and brought the service to an end, the circus owner did not follow his wife back to the camp, but went for a walk across the town. He had not gone far before he picked up the trail of whispers and followed it to the seafront where a small crowd had already assembled at a beach next to the port to watch a group of men, women and children in life-jackets trying to get an old man in a wheelchair out of a rubber dinghy. The crowd grew larger as more came to watch the newcomers struggling knee-deep in the water. They did not ask for help, nor did anyone from the crowd offer. They carried the old man to the beach and sat him in his wheelchair, removed his life-jacket, covered him with a blanket and put a woollen hat on his head. The man who had come to church earlier asked the locals, struggling to make himself understood, where he could buy food and when the next ferry to the mainland was due. When he was told that it might be weeks before it came, he laughed and did not believe it. He asked someone else, looking him in the eye to see whether he would lie to him too, then asked a third and several more but received the same answer, which he repeated to his people. They received the news with yelps and gestures of despair.

The next day there were two tents on the beach and a burning fire, which the new arrivals kept stoking with driftwood. They kept to themselves apart from the occasional visit to the shops, and it was perhaps their discretion more than their plight that made the locals bring them blankets, dry clothes, and old toys for the children. A week later another rubber dinghy appeared, travelling very slowly and being dragged off course by the currents. It was much bigger than the previous one and was loaded down with people, so that its bow and inflatable sides were almost level with the water. It came ashore not far from the two tents on the beach and the earlier arrivals went up to them, but only a few of the newcomers spoke their language. Those who did joined them in their modest camp, while the rest soon bought their own tents, which they pitched some distance down the beach, and the two groups kept out of each other's way.

After a few days, with no sign of the ferry, the travellers finally admitted to themselves that the islanders were telling them the truth. They cleared the beach of their rubbish; they scavenged for firewood and piled it under plastic sheets to dry; they put up washing lines between the trees. Some prayed several times a day, men and women separately, but mostly they passed their time seated outside their tents if the weather was good, chatting in low voices, cooking or strolling through town. Some locals brought blankets and clothes to the latest arrivals too, but also food because there were many who had very little money. This time around the good Samaritans were fewer and the stuff they brought was not quite enough for everyone, but it was still accepted with words spoken in unknown languages and bows of gratitude.

Before very long they lost their shyness and their languages could be heard in the streets and the squares of the town, where they sat on the benches for hours on end and held sometimes heated conversations. Along the esplanade children unconcerned about the cold wind played the games that children play everywhere: football, marbles, hide-and-seek, and a version of tag with teams that took prisoners and threatened them with sticks held like guns. Two weeks later, after a storm that lasted two days, the sky cleared, the sea turned calm and the stranded travellers began to tell each other that surely the ferry would be coming now. The following day, while the good weather continued, a long line of people carrying suitcases, backpacks and small children appeared on the road from the other side of the island. They kept coming all day, making their way towards the town in silence, the flow dwindling to a trickle, then growing again, but never stopping until sunset. They tried not to draw attention to themselves but it was easy to tell them apart from the earlier arrivals because of their wariness and the way they kept close to each other, wandering around the town without asking for directions.

From then on more came every day, getting off boats that landed on other parts of the island during daylight hours. They were crestfallen at the news, shared in their various languages, that they could not travel on to the mainland. After they had accepted their bad luck, the newest arrivals began to look for somewhere to stay. Some could afford to pay for a room in town, and the pensions and small hotels quickly filled up. Others bought tents and pitched them on the beach next to the ones that were already there, but soon the only shop that sold them ran out and the next people to arrive sought shelter in the arcades along the waterfront, under trees and doorways. Eventually even those places filled up and those who came after them slept out in the open under tarpaulins and plastic sheets.

By then no one from the town came to help those arriving. There were more fires burning on the beach and when the travellers ran out of driftwood they stoked them with rubbish and old tyres, but the wind blew the black, acrid smoke towards the town and a policeman came and told them to put the fires out. From then on they only lit small fires to cook and had to keep warm by sheltering in their tents or the arcades or by walking. The streets away from the waterfront filled with them, little groups constantly on the move until night-time when they huddled together somewhere that offered some shelter from the wind. The beach was strewn with empty plastic bottles, drinks cans, cigarette stubs and food wrappings, there was a single tap where everyone lined up to get water, and no toilets they could use.

And they still came from across the sea in ever larger groups, of every age: families with babies, a few very old men and women who were helped along, friends, army deserters with closely cropped hair, some who did not speak the language of any of the others, some who were poor and others less so judging by their clothes and shoes and smartphones, from which they could be parted only in order to have them charged at an unreasonable cost in the coffee shop, which advertised the service with a cardboard sign misspelt in half a dozen languages. They strolled up and down the esplanade, stood at the quay or sat chatting on the beach, staring at the horizon from time to time, waiting for the ferry.

Twelve

SOME DAYS Jamil suffered from a deep sadness, which
he could not explain. If he had been older—or had read
poetry, as the doctor had said when the boy confided
to him (Jamil was not sure whether he was joking)—he
might have recognised the symptoms of melancholy and
understood how defenceless he was against it. But he was
only a child, even though he did not want to be reminded
of that, and the only book of poetry that he knew of, the

poems of Al-Mutanabbi, had never intrigued him enough to take it down from the bookcase at home despite its gold lettering and dusty leather-bound covers.

It was a strange sadness, which he had not experienced before. It did not bring tears to his eyes, even though he had been on the verge the first couple of times it had happened, but it was nevertheless disconcerting. He felt a great weight pressing down on his chest, sometimes hard enough for him to have trouble breathing, but, worse still, he was losing interest in what he happened to be doing at the time: hunting with the catapult, watching the acrobats train or searching futilely for another fossil. He could be feeling quite happy in the morning when he left the caravan, then the next moment his mood would change without anything specific having happened, at least not something that he had noticed, and at a stroke everything in his mind would be replaced by a single, persistent feeling of gloom. What perplexed him about it was that this sadness was not about his mother's or sisters' deaths, or the fact that the ferry had still not come, or that Mokdad spent his time with the circus woman and her elephant instead of him. Those were all sad thoughts, to be sure, but they made him determined, impatient or angry, feelings he understood and fought against. The problem about that other, vague sadness was that it had no obvious cause. He did not know how to fight it off, and for that reason it left him feeling helpless.

The bouts happened without warning, at random times in the day. If the strange mood descended on him in the evening he would take refuge in his bed straight away and sleep it off, after lying awake for what felt like a long time, staring at Mokdad in the dark, not daring to ask to sleep in his bed again, even though it was the only thing that might make him feel better. More often than not the attacks would happen in the morning or the afternoon and last the rest of the day, and he would wander around like a wounded animal, looking for somewhere to hide. The world would close in on him and he would feel as if he was walking through a tunnel that grew narrower as he went, but he could not turn back. Then, after a long time, or the following day sometimes, he would slowly emerge from the dark, again without anything specific having helped him to do so other than sleep and solitude, and become his normal self, although still quite exhausted by what he had gone through.

On some occasions, when the strange mood came over him, he would make the long walk to the town, where he would roam the streets just to keep his mind occupied. That was how he had found out about the new arrivals: he had come to the seafront and seen the makeshift camp on the beach. Since then he had returned to observe them without approaching, even though there were many who spoke his mother tongue. He saw more arriving every day and the fear grew in him that maybe there would soon be more than the ferry could carry and Mokdad and he might have to wait longer if they did not make sure to be in the front of the queue when the time came to go. So he took to going to the town every day, at the time when the ferry would come when it finally resumed its service, and wandering around the waterfront for a few hours, keeping an eye on the horizon, ready to run back to the camp if he saw it coming and fetch Mokdad.

There he noticed a group of boys of various ages, with the ones younger than him following some who were evidently much older. Judging by their accents they all came from the same country as him. From that day on, he looked for them whenever he came to town, and with envy watched them playing football on the beach or trying to fish with makeshift rods. He began to follow them from a distance, through the narrow stone-paved streets around the port, never letting them out of sight, listening to their conversations but not daring to ask them to join in because he saw how they rejected other children who tried to make friends with them. The leader was one of the older boys, perhaps the eldest of them, since he was the tallest and had a shadow of a moustache. His name was Tarek and he was always surrounded by other members of the group, who looked at him with a disciple's eyes and obeyed his commands without hesitation. His physical superiority, however, was not the only reason why he was in charge. He could also speak English, at least well enough to make himself understood with the help of gesturing, and it was he who took their money and bought sweets or cigarettes for the group in the small shop with the caged bird on the esplanade. In the awkwardness with which they smoked, even the older ones, Jamil recognised the newfound sense of freedom that he, too, had felt when he had first arrived on the island, a feeling he had all but lost since, to be replaced, as the weeks passed and the ferry still did not arrive, by the fear of being trapped on that island for ever.

Following them closely (by then the streets were teeming with new arrivals and he could go unnoticed), Jamil listened to Tarek's voice, a deep, deliberately low voice, which forced the other boys to stop and listen carefully as he spoke with an authority that was dented by brief coughs caused by his smoking, to which he was no more accustomed than the others. The older boy sent his vassals on errands, which they rushed to carry out with the satisfaction of having earned his trust, or admonished them for minor transgressions with a couple of words, stern enough to stop them in their tracks and bow a penitent head to him.

Jamil began to come to town earlier every day to shadow the group in such absorption that at times he forgot to look out for the ferry. One morning he could not find them anywhere. They were neither on the beach where he expected to see them at that time of the day, sitting on the sand, waiting until the whole group had gathered before setting off, nor on the quay fishing, nor in the shop with the bird. After an hour of looking for them he came across them in the main square among the other travellers biding their time.

Tarek, taller than the other boys, stood motionless, while the others chased or pushed each other playfully around him. When he grew bored with what they were doing, he snapped his fingers and with a few words punctuated with casual obscenities brought the group to order. Jamil could not help but admire him. He had never been a leader himself—even giving orders to younger children was not something he could do plausibly. He was weak, inadequate, and blaming his parents' strictness for it did not make him any more capable of changing the way he was. He could tell that another boy, shorter than Tarek but sturdier, with black curly hair and dirty clothes, was the second-in-command. His eyes bore none of Tarek's intelligence and he was slow to react when something happened, always looking at his superior for confirmation before roughly grabbing whoever misbehaved and raising his hand to threaten him with a beating.

Apparently everyone was bored. Some members of the group were swinging from the trees, others were chasing the gulls in the square, and some were playing football with a drinks can. While Jamil watched them, as he did every day from a short distance, leaning against a tree, close enough to hear them speak, Tarek turned and rested his gaze on him with a smirk. When their eyes met, the young boy blushed and did not move until the other beckoned him over. Jamil went to him.

'You,' Tarek said in a mocking voice, 'are a spy. You are always around. Staring. Who are you staring at?' He gave him a contemptuous look and Jamil went even more red in the face. After a long silence Tarek burst into laughter. 'Oh, are you going to cry now?' he said.

'No.'

'Yes, you are. How old are you?'

'Eleven.'

'Are you?' the older boy asked with scorn. 'You look more like seven. When did you come here?'

'Two months ago.'

'Liar. I was with the first ones, and we came five weeks ago. You weren't in our boat.'

'We came before you—my father and me. Our boat sank. Only the two of us made it.'

It felt nice to be calling the man his father. The doctor was someone he could be proud of, and it made him sound important, too. None of them would have a father like his. But he ought not to have lied about his age; being young was not something to be ashamed of.

The boy called Tarek said, 'Your boat sank?' He called at the others, saying, 'Did you hear that? His boat sank. Who are you? Sindbad?'

The other children stopped playing and laughed heartily even though they did not quite know why. The group's second-in-command laughed the loudest while giving the unknown boy a look of mistrust, wondering who he was and why he stood so close to Tarek. He listened carefully to Jamil saying, 'My father saved my life. Everyone else drowned. My mother and sisters, too. My father is a doctor.'

'A doctor, eh?' Tarek said. 'You must be rich, then. Buy us something to eat.'

'I don't have much money on me.'

'How much do you have? Empty your pockets.'

Jamil shyly took a few crumpled notes out of his pocket and gave them to Tarek, who counted them before putting them into his. 'Let's go,' he said to the group and they all followed him back to the shop on the waterfront. The money had admitted Jamil to the group and he knew that the circus owner would give Mokdad and him more if they needed it. A few banknotes were nothing to a rich man like the circus owner.

Tarek bought a chocolate bar, which he snapped in two, keeping half for himself and giving the rest to his second-in-command with the order to share it among the group. There was not enough to go around, and a boy complained about the small piece that he was given.

'You give it back,' Tarek said to him. 'You like to talk more than to eat.' His deputy snatched it from the boy. 'Don't speak again,' Tarek said, 'unless it's to say thank you.'

His words were eagerly repeated by his second-in-command and the offender nodded, red-faced. The group walked along the esplanade, with Jamil walking alongside Tarek.

'You're all right,' the older boy said, eating chocolate.

Someone asked, 'What shall we do, Tarek?' and all apart from their leader started talking excitedly.

'Let's go to the beach.'

'What for? There's nothing to do there. Want to go fishing?'

'The fish don't bite. We've been trying for a week.'

'Let's go to the old boat.'

Tarek pondered their suggestion. He had learnt that trick: a leader would not be rushed, he needed time to deliberate and ought to feign disdain. Those habits had served him well. After a moment he said as if doing them a favour, 'All right. Let's go there.'

They came to a place on the shore some distance from the travellers' camp. A wooden fishing boat stood on the beach and the younger members of the group climbed on it and began to rock it, shrieking. Tarek sat down near the water and his second-in-command wandered nearby, glancing back at Tarek who was talking to Jamil.

'I can't stand it, this place,' Tarek said. 'There's nothing to do here. Can't wait for the ferry to come.'

'They say it could be any day now,' Jamil said. 'Where are you going?'

'Germany. You?'

Jamil did not know but said, 'Us too. You have someone there?'

'A brother. Won't recognise him. Haven't seen him in ten years.'

'You travel with your family?'

'Family…' Tarek scoffed. He picked up a pebble and skimmed it across the water.

His lieutenant said from where he stood, 'That was a good one, Tarek.'

'You can come with us,' Jamil said. 'I'll ask my father.'

'The doctor? I don't need looking after. I can take care of myself.'

Then, as though to prove his maturity, he took out the pack of cigarettes and lit one.

Jamil said, 'Can I have one?'

'You smoke?'

'Yes, yes.'

'Does the doctor know?' Tarek asked mockingly.

'No.'

Tarek offered him the packet and the lighter. Jamil tried to light a cigarette without betraying the fact that he had never smoked before. He remembered his father—his real father—smoking and imitated him well enough, he thought, because the older boy did not laugh at him even when he smothered a cough.

'I won't tell your dad,' Tarek said. 'I started smoking when I was your age. How did he save your life?'

Jamil was glad of the chance to talk so that he did not have to smoke. He had always wondered what a cigarette tasted like; now he knew that he did not like it. He said, 'When our boat capsized, he took someone's life-jacket and gave it to me.'

'Did he? What happened to that other man?'

'He drowned.'

'Oh, my mother,' Tarek laughed. 'I never heard of a doctor doing something like that. He's a murderer.'

'He's not a murderer. He did it to save me. And the other one was a bad man.'

'Bad, eh? What had he done?'

'He had let my sisters drown. He didn't let my father help them. We stayed in the water until he managed to push me on to the upturned boat, then climbed on to it, too. We stayed there for a whole day until the sea carried us close to this island. Then we swam ashore.'

Tarek nodded appreciatively. 'Quite an adventure—if it's true.'

'It is.'

The other chortled, but it sounded as if he believed him. 'Where are you staying?' he asked. 'I haven't seen you on the beach.'

'We don't stay on the beach. We have our own caravan.'

'A caravan? How come you've got a caravan? Your father paid for it, right?'

'No, we have no money. We lost everything, but he made friends with a rich man. We can stay with him as long as we want.'

There was no comment. He had failed to impress the older boy so he coyly said what he had been wanting to say all along: 'It's a circus.'

Tarek now took the cigarette from his lips and looked at him. 'What circus?'

'We stay at a circus. It has wild animals and acrobats. It has an elephant, too. You should come and see.'

'Where is it? It's not in town. I haven't seen it.'

'It's not that far.'

'Well, I can't afford a ticket anyway.'

'You don't have to pay. It's not running any shows in winter. You can just have a look around. I'll take you. Show you around.'

Tarek said nothing and began smoking again. He sat near the water, his legs bent, his hand resting on his knee, the cigarette balanced on his lips, looking out at the sea with an aloof expression. Occasionally he took the cigarette from his mouth, tapped the ash to the ground and looked away, trying to stifle the cough of the inexperienced smoker. Other times his fingers searched through the pebbles for a stone to skim, taking confidence from something he was good at. Every time a stone bounced off the surface of the water his second-in-command's voice was heard, exuberant, obsequious, counting the skips. It brought out a frown on the object of his worship. Suddenly Tarek jumped to his feet and brushed off the seat of his trousers. 'Listen up!' he called out. 'Get off the boat. We're going.'

'Where?'

'To the circus. Don't you want to see the circus? My friend here will take us.'

'There's no circus,' the second-in-command said sullenly.

'Yes, there is,' Jamil said. 'Outside of town. I'll show you. It's not too far.'

The sullen boy said, 'What's he saying, Tarek? What circus?'

'He says he lives there.'

'That's stupid. Why does he live in a circus? Is he a monkey?' He turned to Jamil and said, 'You a monkey?'

The others laughed and the older boy beamed with pride at what he had come up with, but the laughter died down when Tarek said, 'Leave him alone, Firas.' He turned to Jamil and asked, 'How far is it?'

'Ten minutes…fifteen.'

'Let's go, then.'

They followed him through the town and on the dirt road to the circus camp. It was afternoon and despite being winter it was a cloudless day, warm enough for everyone to start getting hot after a while. Sweating under his jacket from the brisk walk, feeling thirsty but proud to be guiding the group, Jamil walked on ahead away from the last whitewashed houses of the town. He thought how impressed the boys would be when he showed them around the circus. Afterwards he would introduce Tarek to the doctor with the little speech that he had begun to prepare in his mind: 'This is my father. He is a famous doctor where we come from, but we had to leave when they threatened to arrest him. He speaks English because he studied in England,' he would say. 'He hasn't had the time to teach me yet.' He might then ask Tarek to stay and have a meal with them; he would not ask the other boys to stay, too, even if the circus owner allowed it. Then a troubling thought made him take pause. Would inviting Tarek make the doctor jealous? He would not want Mokdad to think that he was shunning him. He had not stopped loving him despite his sin; he had already forgiven him. No, no, it's a stupid idea, he told himself. He won't like it. I won't ask Tarek to stay.

It was the right decision, and his loyalty to Mokdad gave him a deep pleasure. Love was like that: he no longer shied away from the dreaded word. The image of the two of them together on the deck of the ferry as the island moved away behind them almost brought him to tears. It felt as if his sisters had sacrificed themselves so that he could be happy. He loved them too, very much, but in a different way. He had never felt the fear of losing their love but Mokdad, who had been a stranger only a few weeks before, might stop loving him at any moment. Having earned his love gave Jamil a sense of achievement—an important man like him, taking an interest in an insignificant boy. He thought of his real father with contempt: a crude, uneducated, cruel little man; nothing like the doctor. He wished, he wished… Sometimes his love felt like a burden, and the thought of rejection horrified him.

Firas said, 'Is it still far?'

'No. Perhaps ten, twenty minutes.'

'Twenty? You said fifteen ten minutes ago. I'm not walking another twenty minutes. No, sir. And then we'd have to come back. Let's just not go, Tarek. Let's turn back.'

Jamil said, 'It's a great circus. It has a big elephant.'

'I don't care,' the other said, taking off his jumper. His T-shirt was stained with sweat in the armpits. 'Come on, Tarek. Let's go back.'

Tarek asked Jamil, 'How far is it really? Are we halfway there?'

'Yes. It's up the hill, then…'

'Up the hill?' Firas said. 'Oh, no. I'm not going up any hill. I've already run out of puff. I don't give a toss about the circus. Why did you listen to that fool, Tarek?'

The older boy stood looking at the road ahead, saying nothing. He felt the discontent among his followers, and a hint of doubt that his authority was not indisputable after all worried him. He wanted to see the circus himself, but would not risk losing his command. 'You said it wasn't far,' he told Jamil. 'It's still a long way. We'd better go back.'

His subordinate grinned. 'I bet there's nothing there,' he said. 'An elephant. Yeah, right. We'll be lucky if there are any chickens. Why did you listen to him in the first place, Tarek?'

'Shut your mouth.'

'Sorry. I'm not angry at you. Who is he anyway?'

'His dad's a doctor.'

'I would've needed a doctor if we'd gone all that way.'

There was laughter and Firas grinned with satisfaction again. He had come out of the group leader's shadow and was enjoying the attention. Jamil felt sorry for Tarek. He asked him anxiously, 'Do you want to go hunting?' It was all he could think to say. 'There are always birds in the trees over there.' And indeed the laughter stopped and everyone looked in the direction he was pointing.

'How are we going to shoot them?' Tarek asked. 'Do you have a gun?'

'No, this.' Jamil took out the catapult.

'Did you make it yourself?'

'Yes. You want me to show you how to shoot?'

Firas sneered, 'What, with that? That thing's for little girls.'

'It could kill a bird fifty yards away. Even farther than that.'

'Fifty yards?' Tarek said. 'That thing? Go on, then. Show me.'

They followed Jamil across the field, where he gestured for them to be quiet and loaded the catapult with a stone before approaching the trees alone, wading through the grass softly. When the chirping stopped he stopped too, and scanned the branches. Everyone was silent back where they stood, even his enemy, and his palms felt clammy thinking that he had better not miss with all those eyes on him. After a moment he raised the catapult, stretched the rubber bands and took aim, holding his breath. The stone struck somewhere in the foliage, a small shadow dropped to the ground and the boys gave a loud cheer. Someone hurried to search the grass under the tree and brought back the dead bird, holding it up from its wing. Tarek patted Jamil on the shoulder. 'You aren't useless after all, doctor's boy.'

'That wasn't fifty yards,' Firas said. 'I want to see you killing one from fifty yards.' Then after a moment he said, 'No, give it me. I want to have a go.'

He snatched the catapult from his hand, found a stone and went towards the other trees. Everyone was silent again but did not cheer when he shot. Someone said, 'Firas, you missed.'

'Oh, shut your mouth.'

'Can I have a go?' another boy said.

'No, give it to me,' someone else said.

Firas threw the catapult to them. 'You can have it. It's rubbish. Do whatever you want. I'm going back.'

They turned around and began to walk back towards the road. Jamil watched Tarek go with regret. He was his friend; he wished that he'd stayed a little longer. He had felt great pride when he had impressed him with the catapult. An urge pushed him forward and he caught up with him and said cheerily, 'Do you want to see something?'

'I don't care about hunting really.'

'No, no, something else,' Jamil said and put his hand in his pocket.

'What's that?'

'A fossil.'

The other boy took the strange stone in his hand. 'What's a fossil?'

'It's a thousand years old. Maybe a million.'

'What do you mean, a million? You take me for a fool? It's just an old seashell.'

'I found it in the hills.'

'Yeah, right. I bet you picked it up on the beach.'

'No, no. Don't you see? It's stuck to the stone. They've become one thing.' Tarek raised the fossil to his eyes. 'Once the whole island must have been underwater,' Jamil continued. 'Slowly over the years the land rose up out of the sea.'

While Tarek was studying it in silence, Firas came up to them. 'What's that now?

'A...what did you call it?' Tarek asked.

'Fossil.'

'Let me see,' Firas said, and Tarek let him have it.

'He says the island rose up out of the sea.'

'Did what?' Firas said.

'He found the Lost Atlantis,' Tarek said with a chuckle. 'Tell him, friend.'

Jamil said, 'Give it back.'

'No, I think I might keep it,' his enemy said.

'Give it back!' Jamil said. 'I found it.' Indignation choked him and he reached out to take his treasure from the other boy's hand. Chuckling, Firas evaded his attempts for a while, then, having grown bored with it, hurled the fossil into the scrub.

'Fetch it up!'

Tarek pushed him in the direction of the road. 'Enough, Firas. Let's go. Didn't you say you wanted to get back?'

They went away, leaving Jamil behind, his friend having said nothing to him, his enemy still chuckling. He stood in the field alone, feeling betrayed, weak, a little child dismissed by his elders, watching the group with rage. The bird he had shot lay at his feet, its head twisted backwards, its plumage dusty. He kicked it and felt the tears welling up in his eyes but he was not going to cry; not again, never in his life. He told himself that he was not alone: he had Mokdad. He was his only friend.

They had kept his catapult but he did not care. He would make a better one. It was the fossil that he had to find. He went in search of it where he had seen it land, knelt and rummaged through the grass, unsure whether he was searching in the right place. As the time passed, his fear that he had lost his precious talisman grew, and he began to blame himself for having shown it to Tarek. What a fool he had been to trust him. Only Mokdad had not betrayed him and he missed him now, wanted to be with him; he knew it would make him feel better just to be near him. But he could not go to the camp without the fossil. A cold wind came up and the grey shape of a cloud shrouded the sun, making him stop and zip up his jacket. A sudden fear made him raise his head and look around; there was no one. For the first time it scared him to be alone, and he went back to searching with more urgency, telling himself that the fossil had to be somewhere near. He had been searching for an hour before he decided to try a little farther along, and there he found it in the thick dry grass. He picked it up and rubbed it clean, then, promising himself not to let anyone ever touch it again, he took the road to the camp, holding the stone with the fused seashell tightly in his little helpless fist.

Thirteen

IT WAS SUMMER and Mokdad was on a beach in his swimming costume, wading into the water. The bottom felt muddy, a little like the beach from where they had sailed one night months before, but the water was impossibly warm and offered very little relief from the heat. He took a deep breath and dived in, then swam underwater until he could hold his breath no more and surfaced with a gasp for air, his eyes stinging. He turned and saw that he was already some distance from the shore where Olga waved at him, saying something he could not hear. He waved back and swam towards the open sea for several minutes before he stopped and looked back again. The shore was even farther away now and he could no longer make out the woman. It felt good to be alone for a while. It was as if he were in a hideout, safe and at peace. His mind was free of all anxiety.

The water was cooler there in the deep and his senses welcomed the escape from the hot humid air and the dust. He struck out in another crawl but after a minute gave up, already tired. He thought he ought to return but a heavy swell had begun to gather and made it hard to swim. He made slow progress, stopping to catch his breath every now and then. He was feeling drained, his heart beat hard, his chest hurt, but he did not seem to be any nearer to the shore. The sun always shone and the sea must still have seemed calm from a distance. There was no obvious sign of danger to someone watching from the shore but the swell was coming strongly, carrying him away from the direction he wanted to go. He remembered the circus owner telling him about a woman who had drowned there. Was he going to drown too?

The current pushed and pulled him violently. Panic rose within him and, stretching his neck out of the water, he looked towards the shore. He could not see Olga but desperately waved his arm a couple of times, then stopped: most probably she could not see him either. An absurd sense of embarrassment prevented him from shouting as he struggled on, not looking up at the shore again, moving his arms and kicking with his feet while the water lifted him up and down, up and down, dragging him out into the open sea one moment, sideways the next. It felt preposterous: he had survived the capsizing of the dinghy, only to drown a few hundred yards from the shore.

Suddenly the swell eased and he looked up at the distant beach. The current had thrown him off course and he turned towards the place where Olga must have been, swimming with quick strokes, afraid the swell might build up again. But the sea stayed calm and he made quick progress as he swam head down, eyes shut, taking short, laboured breaths, swallowing water as he went. Finally his feet touched the sand of the sea floor but he still trembled with fear. The woman was not on the beach. He looked for her everywhere. 'Olga!' he called. 'Olga!' But there was no answer. He kept calling until he opened his eyes...

He had received the news of the arrival of the first boat of refugees with a slight nod, just enough to acknowledge that he had heard while keeping a detached expression, as if the information had nothing to do with him, as if he and the travellers stranded in the town were not in the same situation, as if most of them were not his compatriots. By the time they came, he had succeeded in pushing the thought of what had brought him to the island out of his mind most days, but then the travellers had brought his guilt back. He had no wish to see them, or the ones who came after them, each new arrival related to him by the circus owner, who had perhaps sensed something in his guest because whenever he spoke about that particular matter his voice took on a conspiratorial tone. In his latest update he had told Mokdad, 'In any case I understand,' and winked at him. 'You aren't one of them.' Them? What did he mean by it? But the doctor had felt flattered nevertheless.

The only thing that concerned him at the moment was Olga, and in order to be near her he often joined her when she walked the elephant. He would do the same today. It was time to go to the enclosure, where he expected to find her giving Shanti her morning wash. She did not stop him from coming along and he assumed that his company was not unpleasant to her after what had happened, but they had not gone back to the beach with the shipwreck since, or anywhere farther than the fields around the camp where the elephant grazed within sight of the circus tent. Was she afraid to be alone with him? He felt his face flush red and thought that he ought not to go today. He would do something else. Besides, he could be leaving in a few weeks—maybe even in as little as a couple of days if the ferry resumed its service. He had promised Damianos he would stay until summer, but he did not have to keep his word. He was already regretting their deal.

But he knew that he was not really going to leave, not any time soon. The desire to be near Olga, to get to know the woman who had unexpectedly moved him, to listen to her and take pleasure in talking about his life too, would prevent him. He would go to meet her today again after all, he decided. If he delayed he might miss her. He left the caravan.

Olga and the elephant were already walking away from the enclosure and he quickened his pace. Not wanting to appear as though he was running after them, he slowed down before reaching them and put his hands in his pockets before calling out, to give the impression that he just happened to be out on a leisurely walk. The elephant ambled along, pausing to pull clutches of grass with her trunk. The woman said, 'I'm glad to see you. Do you mind having a look at Shanti? Her wound is bleeding again.' She tapped the animal's leg with the guide stick and the animal stopped. Shanti had torn the last of the makeshift stitches and picked at the scab with her trunk, re-exposing the damaged flesh, which was oozing blood and pus again. All Mokdad could do was clean it with antiseptic and reassure Olga that it would still heal but take longer than he thought. The animal resumed her grazing walk and the couple followed her. Olga said amiably, 'Are you looking forward to going away? It shouldn't be long now before the ferry comes.'

How could she say it so casually? he thought, and felt deflated that she would not miss him. Without much thought he said, 'I like it here.'

She did not ask him why but simply said, 'Isn't your plan to go to northern Europe?'

'I'll miss your company, seeing you every day.' He wanted to get a reaction from her and asked, putting his hand on her wrist, 'Do you like me?'

'Yes, doctor, of course,' she said. 'We are friends.'

It hurt him to hear her addressing him with his title. He was reminded of the dream of him drowning, being alone at sea and then alone on the beach. 'Why don't you come with me?' he asked.

'I am married, if you remember,' she said.

'But you don't love him, do you?'

'We have been together for a long time.'

'That doesn't mean anything.'

'It means something to me,' she said with a trace of impatience. 'We have a lot in common. Above all our guilt. We are accomplices to murder. We have to stick together.'

'What happened to your child wasn't your fault.'

'Wasn't it?'

He was still touching her hand; she had not pulled it away. He said very slowly, 'I don't know what happened, but you can't blame yourself for an accident.' He added urgently, 'Come with me, Olga.'

'Haven't you ever lost anyone dear to you?'

'I don't want to lose *you*. You are dear to me.' He said, 'This isn't about what happened on the beach. I wanted you from the first day.'

'You make up your mind about people rather quickly.'

'Don't talk to me as if I'm a child.'

The woman said kindly, 'I'm sure you'll find someone better where you're going, Qasim.'

'I don't have to go. We could live together somewhere in this country.'

'I've thought about leaving him since long before you came. I know it wouldn't work.'

'Was there someone else?'

'Don't you think me capable of taking such a decision on my own?'

'I don't expect you to answer me now,' he pleaded. 'Take your time.'

She withdrew her hand and he felt that she was rejecting him.

'I won't be leaving very soon anyway,' he said, trying
to sound insouciant. 'I have to decide where to go first.
Plan my journey. Your husband said I could stay a little
longer.'

'Oh, Qasim,' Olga said, 'please don't stay because of
me.'

He could not tell her about the deal that he had made
with her husband. He looked away, regretting having
brought the whole matter up. The woman said, 'I am sorry,
Qasim.'

'It's for me to apologise.'

'I'm your friend. I want you to be happy.'

'I suppose if I weren't foreign…'

'It has nothing to do with that.'

But he could not convince himself that it was not one of
the reasons, maybe the main one, and he blamed himself
for it, and the people of the country that he came from. It
was their war not his that had forced him to leave home.
The animal stopped to feed on the branches of a tree and
the doctor wandered off a short distance, staring at the
faraway sea. In another direction the roof of the circus
tent with its coloured flags beating in the wind was barely
visible. The thorn bushes quivered, a few birds crossed the
leaden sky and the repeated sharp noise of twigs snapping
under Shanti's feet punctuated the silence while she fed.
Her serenity was beyond human reach: perhaps only as
a little child had Mokdad experienced such contentment.
Adulthood sets in, he thought, when one realises that one

will never be as happy as that again. And the thought that he had lost something for ever, that there was nothing he could do to regain it, made him feel the weight of time, its slow loss of hope, inevitable and relentless as the decline of the body. Standing only a few feet away, the woman seemed much calmer than him, and for a moment he envied her grief, even though he suspected that it was an illusion, that it was merely the result of her willingness to accept a situation that she could not change. Still he admired her attitude, asking himself whether loss and suffering were the price life extracted for bringing one a little closer to peace.

Someone was coming across the field. Mokdad moved farther away from the woman and faced sea in the distance. Dressed in his white suit, the circus owner waved at them as he strode across the grass. The doctor feigned surprise at seeing him.

'Hello there,' the other man said. 'Enjoying the view, doctor?' His eyes moved from him to his wife, where they lingered before turning back to the foreign man. Mokdad said, superfluously, 'We stopped to let the animal eat.'

'Is everything OK with Shanti?' the circus man said. 'Her wound?'

'She's bleeding a little again.'

'Oh, that's not good, not good at all,' the other said with alarm. 'Olga, what happened?'

'Nothing. She just can't stop picking it. The doctor says she'll be fine.'

Damianos went up to the animal, looked at the wound close up and shook his head in discontent.

'It might take a little longer, that's all,' Mokdad said.

'How long?' the man demanded.

'A few weeks, I should think. There's nothing we can do.'

The three of them had not been together since the day the doctor and Jamil had arrived on the island. Mokdad began to suspect that the man had not come to ask about the elephant. Again he feared that the boy had seen Olga and him on the beach that day and told her husband, but the circus owner gave him no reason to believe it. Besides, he told himself, how would he have told him? Jamil did not speak any English. Relieved, he was on the point of saying something about the animal's injury when the other man pre-empted him. 'Doctor, I come from the town. You are needed. Apparently, it's some kind of medical emergency.'

'How do they know about me?'

'I don't know. I didn't tell them. Someone came up to me and asked whether it was true that a fellow countryman of theirs who was a doctor was staying with me. I couldn't deny it.'

'I suppose I'd better go.'

'They gave me a name to ask for at the camp on the beach.'

Mokdad went reluctantly, not wanting to leave Olga but also not wanting to be among people from home. When he got there the sky had turned darker and the air colder. He made his way to the makeshift camp through the crowd of young people loitering on the esplanade. The first man he asked did not speak his language, but there was a group of his fellow countrymen sitting around a tea kettle on an open fire, and they gave him directions. The man who needed his help thanked him for coming with a bow before leading him to a tent where with much respect he pulled aside the flap and asked him to enter.

In the dark, unlit interior Mokdad made out a large family sitting on a floor laid with flattened cardboard boxes. Several women of various ages dressed in abayas and headscarves, a very old bearded man and a couple of children all stared at him with trepidation, which did not ease after he placed his hand on his chest and greeted them in their common language. When his eyes grew accustomed to the dark, he guessed why he had been asked to come: a birth.

He asked that only one woman stay to help, and waited for a couple of minutes while they argued with each other before losing patience and, surprising himself, snapping at them to decide at once or leave. He had not spoken to anyone like that before, and it felt good for a brief moment to know that he had the right to treat strangers that way, but then he regretted his arrogance, recalling how much he used to despise those of his colleagues whom he had just imitated. Having perhaps noticed his embarrassment, the old man with the white beard made a point of speaking to the women just as sternly, but at the same time in a low, unconvincing voice. He chose the one who would be staying behind himself and ushered the rest of the family out of the tent, kissing the doctor's hand on the way out.

On a bed made of packed holdalls and jackets the pregnant woman, wrapped up in an abaya and a heavy coat, moaned. The scarf that covered her head and neck left a young (perhaps still adolescent) face clear, and a pair of terrified eyes stared at Mokdad. In a calm voice he told her not to worry. He had not expected to use his mother tongue in his profession again. It briefly made him yearn for his old life, but he drove the thought out of his mind and tried to remember what he had learnt in a couple of months of obstetrics at college. The woman could not give birth lying on the bags, but the floor was too dirty to have her lie down, so he asked the older woman who had stayed to help to find some plastic sheets and wash them as best she could. The pregnant woman was shivering.

'Don't be afraid,' he said.

'I'm cold, doctor.'

'Put on one of those jackets.'

He helped her put on one of the jackets covering her makeshift bed. She still moaned, and he helped her try other positions that might make her comfortable until she lay on her side and declared herself all right, even though he could tell that she had only said it to please him.

When the older woman came back, the two of them helped the pregnant woman lie on the clean plastic sheets on the floor, then Mokdad went to ask for soap, clean towels and boiling water. He scrubbed his hands up to the elbow carefully, rinsed them with scalding water and returned to the tent, where the mother-to-be lay under a large flowery tablecloth. She fixed her eyes on him with hope while he explained what he would be doing. She turned to the other woman, who was old enough to be her mother, before giving her consent with a nod, but as soon as he began to lift her dress her hands sought to stop him. He paused and asked impassively, 'Are you still cold?'

'No, no,' she replied and clasped the tablecloth, which covered her, slowly resting her head on the other woman's lap. Mokdad felt sorry for her.

'Have you seen a doctor about the birth?'

This time it was the older woman who replied. 'No.'

'There is nothing to be afraid of,' Mokdad said, and carefully coaxed the young woman into releasing the tablecloth and raising her legs. He pushed the flowery cloth back and lifted her dress. After a quick examination, he asked her to begin to push.

After perhaps an hour she suddenly stopped obeying his urging, covered her legs with the tablecloth and sobbed in the other woman's arms. Mokdad went out to get some fresh air. The family was there, sitting on the sand, the old man fingering a string of amber beads. They all stared at him, apart from the children, who were busy dragging around another child in a wooden box. Mokdad washed his hands in silence, taking his time, and returned inside the tent, where the young woman was not crying any longer. She said, 'Doctor, will he be OK?'

'You know it's a boy?' She shook her head: she only wished. 'There is no reason to worry,' Mokdad said. 'Trust me and be patient.'

They started again. Her cries grew louder and his voice, reassuring at first, became more demanding with time. The light was disappearing and he asked the older woman to get him a torch, preparing himself for several more hours of labour, but while she was gone the baby's head crowned and he knew it would not be much longer. Now he was nervous too, but he tried to control his voice as he spoke to the woman. The baby's head slowly emerged and he eased it out. The cord was wrapped around the neck, and he gently pulled it over the head, then asked for a clean towel and wiped the small purple face. Slowly the shoulders slid out, soon afterwards the rest of the body, and he wrapped the child with towels. It was a girl, and she was not breathing. He began rubbing her back, aware that his hands were trembling, but still could not hear her making any sound. He put her down and with his mouth covering her nose and mouth blew a few gentle puffs of air. Someone was saying something—urgently, demandingly; he did not understand—and he barked out to be quiet, then put his ear close to the baby's face and listened. Just as he was about to try again, she took a breath. He was unprepared for it. He had expected to have to do more to save the baby's life. He would not have been surprised if she had died: tragedy belonged in this wretched place. But her little soft body stirred and she opened her eyes, and he burst out laughing with exhilaration.

He came out of the tent into the early evening. The camp was dark under the overcast sky and a small crowd of strangers had gathered. He was patted on the back, kissed on the forehead and a roll of banknotes was pressed into his hand. He had to refuse it several times before it made its way through several hands back into the old man's pocket. He accepted a glass of spicy tea to celebrate the baby's birth, shook every hand offered to him before making his excuses, but they would not let him go, summoning him back for another glass of tea. He relented several times, until his weariness prevailed over his good humour and resisted their endless pleas to stay.

Mokdad walked along the esplanade away from the beach. A group of men talked in an incomprehensible language, a pair of policemen walked with a swagger and the glass globes on the street lamps glowed with yellow light. Men coming the other way, some holding hands, stared at him with curiosity. They had not seen him around before; they assumed he had just arrived. A rowdy crowd of children laughed and pretended to push each other into the water. It could have been an evening at home before the war. Dusk fell; there was no moon and he would be walking back to the camp in the dark. A fight broke out somewhere: young men exchanging blows while others watched as though it were a performance. The violence was not enough to shake off the boredom of another day passing without the ferry coming. Something fluttered noisily by, passing close to his head—a bat, perhaps—and he felt the draught of its wings on his face. His exhilaration was already gone.

A group of children who spoke his language were engrossed in shooting at a tree with a catapult. 'Doctor,' a voice said, 'doctor.' People stopped and watched. He looked back over his shoulder and saw the old paterfamilias of the household with the newborn waving at him. He waved back, even though the man's gesture was clearly a request for him to wait. And indeed, the man began to walk towards him, but Mokdad turned and went on at a brisker pace while the other kept calling after him,

'Doctor, doctor, wait a minute,' in his feeble respectful voice, silencing everyone on the esplanade. Even the children had stopped playing with the catapult and were staring at him. Mokdad stopped and waited for the old man to catch up. He pressed something into Mokdad's hand. 'Take it, take it,' and the doctor felt the roll of banknotes he had refused several times already. 'You're a good man.' This time he accepted the money to put an end to the spectacle and quickened his step, turning into a street off the waterfront where he could no longer be seen, but a sense of shame, when he ought to have been pleased with what he had done that day, followed him to the circus camp, to the caravan, to his bed.

Fourteen

IT WAS THE MOST powerful catapult Jamil had ever made, shaped out of a thick dried-out oak branch, which he had picked up on one of his walks in the fields far from the town, where he no longer went much from fear that he might come across the boys again. He had spent many hours working on it, had even sanded down the wood and lacquered it, until he was pleased with the result and no longer regretted having had the old one stolen from him. But he had not forgotten what the boys had done, nor forgiven them. If he was going to town today it was only because he had to ask about the ferry. It was the second week of calm seas in the middle of winter, the time of year that if he had grown up in the country he would have identified as the halcyon days, regular as the solstice. The ferry was bound to come now.

On the way he tried the catapult, shooting it at the road signs and prickly pears, taking pride in his creation, which he declared more accurate than his previous one, the one stolen from him. He loved to hold it in his hand, run his fingers over it and admire it; it was proof in his eyes that he was not an inept little boy but capable and wise beyond his years. Suddenly he saw a group of people ahead. Was it the boys? He quickly hid the catapult in his jacket and for a moment, his heart pounding, he considered leaving the road and going into the fields to avoid them, but a sense of pride stopped him despite his fear and he walked on with his head bowed and his hands in his pockets.

He was still some distance away when he realised that it was not them but another group of younger boys, whom he haughtily ignored when they spoke to him. For a while afterwards he felt emboldened, ready to face down his enemies, but when he reached the first houses of the town his swagger gave way to a hesitant walk, which guided him with prudence through the quieter back streets where he was unlikely to come across them. He braced himself for seeing them in the seaside camp, where he was hoping to learn news of the ferry, but as soon as he came to the waterfront he saw that there were no tents or people on the beach, only strewn rubbish, torn tarpaulins and the charred remains of open fires. Instantly the thought that they had left on the ferry terrified him and he dashed along the esplanade towards the port, already convinced that it was too late. He was still some distance away but he ought to be able to see the ferry—the fact that he could not meant that it was already gone. And yet he ran senselessly on until the quay came into full view, and then a rush of relief took hold of him. The people from the camp were all there, with their luggage, clustered along the quay. Someone said that the ferry was coming, praise be to God, that it was expected a couple of hours later, which was barely enough time for Jamil to hurry back to the circus camp and tell Mokdad.

Even though he had been expecting the ferry to arrive any day now, it still felt like the most exhilarating piece of news. He was leaving the island at last, taking the doctor away from that woman. It would be just the two of them from then on. His breast still hurt with love at the thought of their time together at sea many months earlier. If God had sent Mokdad to look after him, there had to be a divine explanation for their long stay on the island, too. He remembered the Koran lessons with the imam in the mosque: how God had created a world of trials and tests for people. Maybe God had kept the doctor and him there to test them. There was no greater temptation for a man than a woman, as the Prophet had said, and Mokdad had failed it. But the ferry was coming now, and everything would be fine. They were alive, God would forgive the man, and everything Jamil had hoped for would come true. Jamil had asked God to forgive his friend before and he asked Him again. A happy life opened up before the two of them.

Was the camp really so far away? He was already out of breath, but he could still see the houses of the town behind him. He had to walk faster.

He made it to the camp panting and sweating, not knowing what time it was, hoping that Mokdad had not left with the woman and the elephant for their walk. He felt a thrill of anticipation as he imagined the doctor receiving the news with as much delight as he had. It would be wise to avoid going by the woman's caravan. If she saw him she might guess why he was in such a hurry. He did not trust her not to want to keep Mokdad there. As he made a detour around it he could feel himself being watched by the circus hands and he slowed down and avoided their eyes. He hoped the doctor would still be in their caravan. There might not be enough time to make it to the port if he was gone. And then—he did not want to think about it.

He opened the door to the caravan: the man was there, shaving. Jamil was barely able to check his excitement as he said, 'Uncle, uncle!'

Mokdad kept staring into the small mirror propped up against the counter of the kitchenette and continued to shave. He said calmly, 'What is it?' and dipped his razor into a bowl of water.

'The ferry. It's coming.'

'Ah,' Mokdad said. 'Right. Someone said it might be coming today.' He began shaving his upper lip, bending forward to see better in the mirror. A zebra brayed somewhere and Jamil quickly looked out: no one was coming. The doctor said, 'Those people sleeping out there on the beach will go now.'

Jamil said anxiously, 'It's coming now. In an hour. It won't be staying long.'

'No, I shouldn't think so. Have you been running?'

'We have to hurry up. Come. Let's go.'

The doctor said, 'Sit down. Don't worry. The ferry will come again. It'll be coming every week from now on.'

'No, not next week. Why? We have to go now. Today.'

Jamil began to gather their few belongings furiously: the clothes they had borrowed, a holdall the circus man had given them. He said to the face in the mirror, as if Mokdad had not heard, 'Be quick. We have to go. There isn't much time. We'll have to run.' He stood tapping his foot, waiting.

Mokdad said, 'The ferry can't possibly take everyone. There'll be too many before us in the queue.'

'We have tickets, remember?'

'Calm down. Don't get excited. There's no hurry.'

He finished shaving and washed his face with slow, deliberate movements. Half an hour must have passed since Jamil had been in town. They could still catch the ferry if they ran. Perhaps Mokdad knew exactly when the ferry was coming, Jamil thought; perhaps the circus man would give them a lift in one of his lorries.

The doctor said, 'Our host…' then, after a moment's hesitation '…asked us to stay.'

'Here? Today?'

'He asked us to stay a little longer. A few weeks perhaps.'

'Why?'

'He needs us.'

'I don't want to stay. What does he want from us?'

'He's been very good to us. If it weren't for his wife and him…'

'No. He can't make us stay.'

'We would be ungrateful,' the doctor said. 'He wants my help with the elephant. The animal isn't well.'

'What's wrong with it?'

'She's injured. I have to get her well.'

'It's not ill,' the boy said. His little dark eyes stared suspiciously at him. 'You lie.' He shifted uneasily and looked around the caravan.

'You've seen her wound,' Mokdad said, 'haven't you?'

'It's not your fault, is it?'

'All the same, I have to make sure she gets well. We owe it to the people here who helped us.'

'He can't force you. What would he have done if you weren't here? He wants to trick you. He wants to make you work for free. If he were a good man he'd let us go. We have a long way to go. We've been here for so long. You promised we'd go.'

The doctor said slowly, 'The man has been very good to us and wants to help us. More than me, he wants to help you. He's told me how much he likes you. His wife likes you, too. Don't you like her, Jamil?'

'No, I don't like her. She's not my friend.'

'Don't say that. She let you ride the elephant.'

'I don't like the elephant,' Jamil said stubbornly. 'I want to go.'

'To go where? You don't know if you'd like it in another country. This place—not just this island, the whole country—isn't that much different from home, is it? They live pretty much like us.' He went on, 'You'll have everything you wish for. They'll look after you and you'll learn the language, go to school.'

'I don't like it here. I hate this place.'

'You aren't going to stay on this island,' Mokdad said. 'They'll leave in the summer. They'll go back to the mainland.' He touched the boy on the shoulder. 'They are good people.'

Jamil listened broodingly, holding the packed holdall.

'It wouldn't be any different in the north. In fact it could well be worse. I've been thinking about it. You wouldn't have anyone to take care of you over there.'

'I'll have you.'

'Me, me! That's not what we agreed, is it?'

'You promised to take me there,' Jamil said, 'you did.' He stood there demanding an answer, but what he really wanted was to touch Mokdad, tell him that he loved him and beg him to go, convince him how happy he would make him if only the two of them left now.

Mokdad washed his razor and put it away. 'You have to understand—'

'No, we have to go. We'll be late. We'll take the path that goes behind the caravans; they won't see us. We could say we're—'

Mokdad made a gesture of exasperation. 'No. I don't think it's possible.'

They would not be leaving that day. What remained

of Jamil's exhilaration drained from his body, leaving him exhausted. He had a quick thought: there was no reason to leave the country, after all. Mokdad was right. It could be a good place to live—as long as they were nowhere near the circus couple. His face brightened with hope and he said, 'I'll stay if you do too.'

The zebra had not stopped braying outside. A circus hand hurried past the caravan window and Jamil heard him calling out something sharply in the rough, incomprehensible local language. Mokdad said, 'I can't stay.'

The boy took hold of Mokdad's shirt and said, 'You said we can't leave.'

'I meant for a couple of months. Then I'll go, and you'll stay with them. They are good people. They'll treat you like a son. They want to have a child.'

Mokdad stopped talking but Jamil said nothing. He was thinking that he ought not to cry. He wouldn't cry; he was not a little child. He had promised himself never to cry again. At last the doctor said, 'Listen. I don't have any money. I lost everything in the crossing, didn't I? How am I supposed to take care of you?'

'I'll get a job.'

'*You'll get a job.*' Mokdad chuckled and Jamil flushed with anger. He could feel his face burning and he turned his back to the man to hide it. Mokdad said, 'You don't know me any better than you know them. At your age you'll learn their language very quickly, you'll see.'

'I want to be with you. We are friends.'

'We'll always be friends. I'll write to you.'

Jamil fell silent again. There was so much to think about. What was he going to do? He did not know; he felt helpless like, like…a child. He asked with piteous hopefulness, 'We'll go to the mainland?'

'Yes, yes, of course. In the summer. I…might go earlier myself.'

The evasiveness of the answer horrified Jamil and he began to bite his nails. The doctor said, 'We can't carry on living like this. The caravan is too small for both of us. When I go, you'll have it to yourself.'

'No, no. I'd rather be with you. There is plenty of room.' He was short of breath and his heart thumped as he persisted. 'I don't want to be alone.'

'You won't be alone,' Mokdad said. 'You'll have them. They'll be like a father and mother to you.'

'I have a father back home.'

'You never said… Would you rather go back there?'

Jamil frantically shook his head: that would have been worse. 'You promised to travel with me,' he said, 'you promised to take me to that country in the north, but now you'll go alone and I'll stay here.'

'It was wrong to promise you,' the doctor said. 'I am sorry. I shouldn't have agreed in the first place. I can't take care of you.'

Why was God doing this to him? Was it a test he had to endure? He said, 'It's a sin to break a promise.'

The boy's piousness made Mokdad smile.

'I am sorry.'

Was he making fun of him? No, no, it could not be. He was a good man and loved him as much as he loved him.

Mokdad said, 'If you don't stay with them, the police will put you in an orphanage, you know.'

'I can take care of myself.'

'It makes no difference. It's the law. A child your age can't travel alone. Even if we went together, I wouldn't be able to stop them from taking you away from me.'

'We'll tell them you are my father.'

'And do we have any papers to prove it?'

'We'll find a way,' Jamil said obstinately.

'And if you stay here you'll be able to do as you like.'

'If you don't let me come with you I'll go alone,' Jamil said suddenly. 'I don't need your help. And I'll find someone else to tell the police he's my father.'

'You shouldn't do that. There are bad people…'

Jamil regretted what he had said but could not take it back now. If he scared the man enough he might make him change his mind. He slung the holdall over his shoulder and said, 'I'm going. The ferry is on its way. If you don't come now you'll miss it.'

'Don't be a fool, Jamil.'

'No, you can't stop me.'

Mokdad stared at him. Could he tell that he did not mean it? He would leave alone if he did not come—he was going to leave, Jamil told himself, feeling unbearably sad. It was worse than the time right after his sisters had died. He had had the man back then; now he was truly alone. Why was God doing that to him? Was it because he never prayed? He decided to make a deal with Him. If He made Mokdad come with him, Jamil would start going to the mosque and pray and do all the things the imam used to say. The months that the man and he had spent together on the island had been the happiest time of his life. It was over now. There was nothing to look forward to. But he could not stay. There was still a chance Mokdad would follow him if he loved him. And he did love him, Jamil was convinced that he did, despite what he had just said.

He repeated with feigned assurance (he felt his hands trembling), 'I'm going,' then stood holding the door open.

'Good luck.'

'You should hurry if you want to catch the ferry.'

'Come back if you change your mind,' Mokdad said.

'No, I won't,' Jamil said harshly.

He left the caravan and made his way across the camp expecting to hear Mokdad's steps behind him, but he got to the dirt road without anyone following him. The fact that he was free to leave unnerved him, but nevertheless he went on at a faster pace, still convinced that it would not be long before the doctor caught up with him. A few minutes later, unable to resist any longer, he looked back: no one was coming after him. He gave way to despair and began to cry. He had said he would never do it again but the more he thought about his vow of adulthood the more he sobbed, until he thought that the only way to stop it would be to run. He started running as fast as he could, and, sure enough, he soon stopped crying and the air against his face dried his tears. Still he kept on running. He could not stop now; he was tired from having run on that road in the opposite direction only a short while before, but he was not going to slow down. He was not going to miss the ferry.

He was halfway to town when he saw, far in the distance, the big white ship entering the bay, a long trail of black smoke stretching low behind it. He tried to run even faster than he already was but was soon gasping for breath and had to slow down, reassuring himself that he would still be there on time. Going downhill, he could not see the ship any more, but two blasts of its horn travelled all the way to him. He imagined it coming into port at that moment, but he was not far, he could see the town ahead. When he came to the seafront the ferry was manoeuvring with its stern towards the quay and the crowd was pressing together and edging forward. He tried to push his way through but could not make it farther than those at the very back. A scuffle broke out between two national groups but stopped when a man in uniform corralled the crowd to the side of the quay, from where they watched as the ferry tied up and lowered the ramp at its stern.

The crowd moved forward again. Jamil could not see over the people in front of him, but the voices were becoming more excited, giving God thanks or swearing or bursting into laughter. He thought of the doctor and looked for him all round but he was not there, and Jamil stopped believing that he would come. The wind blew the diesel fumes from the ferry's funnels across the quay, the rough sea swayed the ship, the hawsers looped around the bollards stretched and the crowd carried the boy forward. Soon he would be gone. The piece of land he had been so eager to flee felt like home now and he was touched with fear at the thought of leaving it. Was he a little child after all who could not take care of himself? At the camp he had felt great sorrow when Mokdad had told him to stay with the circus couple, a betrayal he had not expected from him, an act so unexpected that the thought of it almost brought him to tears again. But the thought he found harder to bear as he stood on the quay was that he would never see Mokdad again. The island where he had stayed with him for the past months, in a small caravan where he had so many times secretly watched him sleep, unable to sleep from the restlessness of love himself, would for ever be the last place that they had been together.

When the crowd moved again, he was pushed from behind and blindly shuffled forward. The thought that the boys who had stolen his catapult and made fun of him would be among the people waiting to board worried him, no matter how much he told himself that he did not care if they saw him. If Mokdad had been there... He thought of him still being in the camp, where he would find him if he turned back now. No, he could not go back. If he did, the circus man and his wife would not let him leave again. His mind seethed with suspicion and the fairy tales he had heard when he was very little: a poor orphan, kept prisoner by an evil couple, who must toil to earn his living.

The pushing eased and through the people in front of him he saw the man in uniform on the stern ramp checking the travellers' documents before letting them board. Jamil handed him his ticket and the man had a look at it, then asked something in the local language. Jamil had only a couple of words in it. He began to say, 'Yes, yes,' gesturing in the direction of the ferry, but the uniformed man asked him something incomprehensible again, raising his voice.

What did he want? There should not be a problem with the ticket: the doctor had bought it for him. He knew one more word in the foreign language and began to repeat it like a prayer, 'No, no, no,' then made an attempt to walk up the ramp, but the man grabbed him by the shoulder and held him back. A woman's voice behind Jamil said something and the boy recognised the sound of English, which the doctor spoke. The man in uniform let him go, but Jamil did not dare attempt to climb on to the ramp again. The woman said in Jamil's mother tongue, 'Where are you from?'

He stared sullenly at her.

'Where's your family?'

'I don't have anyone.'

'You came all this way on your own?'

'Yes.'

'Where are you going?'

He tried to remember the name of the country Tarek had mentioned. 'Germenay.'

The woman grinned and he looked away infuriated, expecting to be made fun of, but she said, 'That's where I'm going too, but you need papers.' He stood biting his nails under the stares of the crowd and tried to think of a lie that would get him on to the ferry. If the doctor had been there he would have known what to do. The woman said, 'Do you have a passport?' and appalled him by stroking his face. He blushed and pushed her hand away and became aware of laughter around him. The woman asked, 'Do you know what a passport is?' He nodded, while the people waiting to board the ferry started to get impatient. 'What is your name?' but he did not answer her. 'Don't you want to tell me your name, darling?'

'I want to get on the boat. I have a ticket. I'm going to Germenay.'

'Well,' the woman said, 'they won't let you get on the ferry without papers.'

'I lost them,' he said, and looked at the ship he was not allowed to board.

'Don't worry. The police will make new ones for you,' the woman said. She put her hand on his shoulder and pulled him cautiously away from the man in uniform. 'You can't travel otherwise,' she said in a lower voice. 'You'll have to tell them your name. And say you have family where you're going.'

'And then they would let me get on the boat?' Jamil asked.

She talked to the man in uniform and turned back to the boy. 'Not today. It's a lot of work. The next time the ferry comes. Maybe.'

He wanted to tell her that he could not stay on the island another day. He could not go back to the camp: Mokdad did not want him and the circus couple would not let him leave again. But he could not say it, not in front of all those people standing around, staring at him. He would be making a fool of himself.

The woman spoke to the man in uniform again and told the boy, 'He says to wait for him in the police station,' and gave him directions. He walked away from the intent eyes watching him, making his way through the crowd with his head bowed, away from the ferry and the quay, to return to the camp, which he'd thought he would never see again.

Outside the town he left the road and walked across the fields, striding through the dry brush at a fast pace. It had rained the night before and soon his trousers were wet up to the knees, but he walked on, dour and determined, his young face set in a scowl, his hair uncombed, alone, carrying the large holdall. His legs hurt from all the running he had done that day and he paused to catch his breath. He stared at the landscape he had first seen when he had walked with Mokdad, both of them still wet through, from the beach to the circus camp: the green and grey fields with thorn bushes and a few trees growing among the rocks, a landscape that was not dissimilar to the place he had grown up but which he now hated more than home. All his fond memories of his time on the island were of Mokdad; everything else had blended into a haze of discontent. A blast of cold wind revived his agitation and, feeling bold, he had the urge to hurry back to the camp.

He went straight to his caravan, where he was greeted by the pair of narrow beds, the broken kitchenette, the tin floor—and silence. He should not have expected the doctor to be there; he would still be out with the elephant and the woman. He sat on the edge of Mokdad's bed and put his hand on the pillow, then lay down and buried his face in it. The man's smell was enough to make him feel safe and calm. When would he get back? He needed to speak to him. He remembered how he had got into Mokdad's bed one night in their first few days on the island but the man had sent him back. It hurt to think of all the little rejections he had suffered. Perhaps they had been his fault.

He could not stay lying for long; his body throbbed with a wild energy. He could not wait for Mokdad to return. He needed to speak to him right away, needed to find a way to convince him to leave with him the following week. It was quiet outside: circus hands working on repairs or tending the animals. He saw the owner walking up to one of the workers and talking to him, then walking away from the camp, on the road to the town. He was suddenly reminded of truanting and the excitement of skulking around the streets near school. A teacher had caught him once and beaten him with a switch, then marched him home, where his father had done the same with his belt, but Jamil had gone back to doing it again. He hated school but he would promise Mokdad to go if he came with him. He would keep his promise. He wanted the doctor to be proud of him. He would do anything he asked him to. He left the caravan and went across the camp, expecting a voice to call out to him in the rough unfriendly language he did not understand, but no one spoke.

Had they noticed him? Would they later remember seeing him walking across the camp? It was one of the few advantages of being a child: adults paid very little attention to him. But he could not be certain, so he made a point of walking on the road to the town until he was out of sight of the camp, and then he returned through the fields, taking care not to be seen, going to the back of the circus owner's caravan. The windows were half open. He had to be careful—assume the woman was in, even though in all likelihood she would be with the elephant. He lifted a window carefully and, pulling himself up, peered in. No, there was no one in, he was quite sure. He needed to fetch a box and step on it in order to climb in. Once inside he closed the window, drew the curtains and stood without touching anything. The clean floor, the laundered sheets, the humming of a refrigerator were the sorts of things he would never notice at home, but now they struck him as extravagant luxuries, as though the couple did not have the right to live like that while his friend and he lived in squalor. In the wardrobe an elaborate outfit hung on the rail, and he moved aside the other clothes to have a look: a red riding jacket with gold braids and epaulettes. With it hung a pair of white trousers, and in the bottom of the wardrobe a pair of patent leather boots. It was the way he imagined an army general's uniform would look, if it were not for the black top hat next to the boots.

There was noise outside and he cowered, his heart racing, but it was only a worker carrying something past. After he was gone, Jamil resumed his search. From the wardrobe he moved to a chest of drawers and there he found what he was searching for: a strongbox in the back of the top drawer, hidden behind the folded clothes. It was heavy, and locked. It must contain money: he had never seen the woman wearing jewellery. He found a knife and carried the steel box to the bed, where he tried to prise it open. The knife bent but he kept pushing it into the slit under the lid, not wanting to accept that he could not get to the money. Finally he gave up, put the box back and went back to searching the rest of the caravan. He retained some hope that he might find more money hidden elsewhere.

There was none, but in the bedside table he found a set of keys, and he quickly took out the strongbox again and began trying them in the lock. While he did so, he was praying with true piety. God understood that Mokdad and he needed the money much more than the owner of the circus. Again he promised God that he would change, he would become a good Muslim if only He would help him now. Then one of the keys slid into the hole, turned without resistance and the lid popped open. There was a thick wad of banknotes inside and Jamil took it into his hands. He assumed it was a lot of money, which ought to last them until they reached their destination. He imagined showing it to Mokdad. How happy he would be; he would have no reason not to take him with him now.

He put the wad in his pocket and returned the strongbox to its place. He did not have to worry about what the circus owner would do when he found out that the money was missing; anyone in the camp could have taken it. There would be no way to prove that Jamil had done it as long as he hid it carefully somewhere. He should go now: he had found what he had come for. But he could not bring himself to leave. Perhaps there was more money, and he might not have the chance to return. He looked through the rest of the caravan. There was a piano whose keys he did not dare touch, and an album with old photographs of a young girl. And there were food tins in the cupboards and a box full of books with illustrated covers—adventure novels, he could tell that much.

There was no more money but still he did not want to go. The clean sheets and the clothes on the rail and the photo album stopped him from leaving. He lay on the bed and shut his eyes. He did not want to return to his dirty, small caravan.

There was a knock on the door and he jumped up, thinking that he had been caught. While he was trying to decide what to do, there was another urgent rap. He hoped that the door was locked, that God would protect him. He began to pray silently: 'In the name of God, the infinitely compassionate and merciful...' while standing still. A blurred human shape was framed by the door window. '...Lord of all the worlds...' There was nowhere to hide, no room under the bed or the wardrobe, he had searched those places already. '...Guide us on the straight path, the path of those who have received your grace...' The shadow disappeared from the frosted glass and Jamil breathed again.

He did not linger any longer. He made his way out through the same window and ran into the brush, his pocket bulging with the money. The exhilaration of having carried his plan through drove him on, away from the camp. He was free now; he could leave the island with Mokdad. He was glad that he could do something for him, too, with the money that he got. There was no guilt in his thoughts. It had all been the circus man's fault, who wanted to keep him on the island.

He was feeling strong again, no longer like a child. He did not want to go to his caravan, where he would be alone. Oh, how happy he was, he thought, and said it aloud several times. His voice travelled far in the quiet of the fields, sounding as though it belonged to someone else, someone who was truly happy. He had the urge to tell Mokdad right away, let him see the money, but would have to be careful not to be seen by the woman. He could not wait to make the doctor happy, as happy as he was. And yet, despite his exuberance, a little blemish coloured his thoughts, as he wondered whether the doctor might not like what he had done after all. Strictly speaking it was theft, he told himself, but dismissed the accusation with the argument that the circus owner was very rich and would easily make back the money, while for the doctor and him it was their only hope.

A cold wind was blowing, the dry bushes shook, and the air was filled with the smell of wet earth. Walking quickly, squeezing the banknotes in his pocket, shivering with cold but still smiling, Jamil searched in every direction for the elephant. After more than an hour, unable to find the animal and the two people, he took the road back to the camp. When he was almost there he saw them up ahead, making their way back, too. He did not approach them. He had to wait for Mokdad to be alone before speaking to him. He trailed them with a growing fear that they might do something sinful again. Kissing or holding each other in their arms felt as depraved to him as what he had watched them do on the beach. But they did nothing of that sort. They walked side by side, not too close to each other, following the elephant. Still Jamil's joyfulness faltered. He stopped thinking of what he wanted to tell the doctor and his reaction when he showed him the money; now he was only thinking of the woman, and his jealousy and mistrust flared up. He felt a great urge to save Mokdad from her. He could do it because on this occasion he was stronger than him. The woman could not seduce him; he felt only contempt for her.

He walked behind them, slowing down if he thought that he was getting too close, hiding behind the tall shrubs when they paused. When they reached the camp he was still following them, waiting for the woman to leave before he approached Mokdad, but then she turned round and saw him. She waved at him and he had no option but to go to them. She said something to him with a smile, which the man did not translate.

'Well,' the doctor said to Jamil in their language, 'you didn't leave after all.'

'I need papers.'

'You can't travel alone. I told you so.'

'The police said I can get papers,' Jamil said. Out of the corner of his eye he could see the woman stroking the elephant and checking its wound. It was of some consolation to know that he could communicate with Mokdad in a language that she could not comprehend. In his presence he never felt weak. He said, 'Can we go now?' growing impatient again. 'I need to speak to you.' He touched the money in his pocket, tempted to pull the wad out and show it to him.

'I have to help with the animal,' the doctor said.

He told the woman something in English and started walking again. The boy followed them. 'I have something I must tell you,' he said.

191

'Go on, then, say it,' Mokdad said and took a long breath. 'If it's so important.'

The elephant stopped to pull out clumps of grass, which she ate after brushing them carefully against the ground to clean away the dirt. The doctor gave the child a tolerant look. 'So, what is it, then? Did you hear something in town?'

'We can leave now.'

'I said I have to help with the animal.'

'No, no. I mean leave the island. You don't have to worry any more. I took care of it.'

'What did you do?'

'I've found some money.'

'Where did you find it?' Mokdad asked sharply.

Jamil hesitated: it was not what he had expected. He said, 'The man from the circus gave it to me. For our journey. We can go together now, yes?'

'Show it to me.'

'Here. Look,' Jamil whispered. He took out the wad and held it with both hands. Shanti started to walk again and Olga followed her, but Mokdad stood there, staring at the money in the boy's hands. 'Be careful,' Jamil said. 'Don't let her see it.'

'Why not? Where did you get it?'

'It's ours. He gave it to me. I promise. He told me not to let her know.'

Mokdad said, 'Let me see it. You'd better be telling the truth.'

'I promise. I'd never…'

'Let me have it,' the man said.

He turned to the woman, who had stopped up ahead waiting, and called out, 'Please carry on. We'll catch up.'

'Sure, Qasim.'

The doctor turned back to Jamil. 'She's leaving. Now show me.'

The boy held the money out to him. 'Is it enough to last us the rest of the journey?' he asked.

Mokdad thumbed cursorily through the wad but said nothing.

'It must be enough,' Jamil said. 'We could stay in a hotel and eat in restaurants. We won't have to ask anyone for help again. And we could travel alone, we won't have to join the others.'

The doctor shook the money in his face. 'Do you think I'm a fool?' he said. 'I know you stole it. This is a lot of money. If he'd wanted to give it to us he wouldn't have given it to you. Where did you get it from? Tell the truth. Did you go in their caravan?'

'I didn't take all of it. There's more. He's rich. It's not a lot to him.'

'You went into their caravan and stole the money. What else did you take?'

'Nothing, nothing,' Jamil said, 'I only took what we need. He would've let us have it if we'd asked, wouldn't he?'

Mokdad slapped him. Jamil had been slapped countless times and it normally meant nothing to him, but he was not expecting it from Mokdad. He looked up in astonishment.

'You will go straight to their caravan,' Mokdad said, 'and put it back. Do you hear?'

'I can't,' Jamil said, 'they might see me. Don't worry, no one knows it was me. I was very careful. They don't need the money, really. They have lots. We need it; how else are we going to get where you want to go? I'm a good Muslim; I wouldn't do anything bad.'

The woman and the elephant were already some distance away. The air was cold; it was probably no more than three in the afternoon, but it was already turning dark. Mokdad said, 'Why did you do this? These people have been good to us.' He still held the money with an angry fist.

'I don't want to stay here with them,' Jamil said, looking at the hand holding the money. How unfair it was to be blamed for having tried to help not just himself but Mokdad too. He had taken a big risk. The man's ingratitude stirred up an unexpected hatred in him. He was surprised by it. He tried to chase it away from his thoughts. He said, 'I want us to leave together. I want us to be together. I'll never do it again. I'll be good, I promise. Please don't leave me with these people.'

'Don't talk to me about that again. Do what you like. I think it'd be best for you if you stayed. When you're old enough to understand… But go if you want. I'm not going to stop you. Did I stop you from leaving this morning? Go. But not with me. No, no, no. I'll be going alone.'

The boy reached out and touched his hand. 'Please, please. Qasim.'

Mokdad pulled his hand away. He said angrily, 'I don't want to travel with you. Leave me alone. Don't you understand?'

'Don't say that. We're friends. Please. I won't be any trouble. Let me come with you. Don't leave me here.'

'Stop it. You hear? Stop all that. I'm not your friend. Give the money back and leave me alone.'

'No, Qasim. No.'

The man looked at the elephant and the woman getting farther away. He regained his composure and said quietly, 'Come. Let's go now.'

He went ahead, in a hurry to rejoin the woman. How Jamil hated her for what she had done to Mokdad. He said without much thought, 'If you don't let me come with you I'll tell him.'

Mokdad stopped and looked back. 'Tell who? What?'

'The man from the circus. I'll tell him about the woman and you.'

'What the hell do you mean?'

'I saw you. That day on the beach.'

Mokdad came back and slapped him again, harder than before. Anger welled up inside Jamil and this time he did not try to check it. He said determinedly, 'I'll tell him, I'll tell him.'

Mokdad looked at him. 'How? You don't speak his language.' He turned and walked away from Jamil. He said with his back to him, 'I'll keep the money until we get back to the camp. Then we'll go and find him together. You'll give the money back and say you're sorry. I'll ask him to forgive you.'

He caught up with the woman when they had almost reached the camp, leaving Jamil some distance behind. The doctor said something to her, which made her laugh.

What had he told her? Was it about him? Jamil felt a guiltless hatred for her and kept his distance while still following them. It was her fault that Mokdad had behaved like that. Had she told his friend anything about him? The idea flashed through his young mind that she had used magic on him. The imam had talked about sorcery once, how it was one of the tricks that Satan used to lead people astray. And hadn't he heard his sisters talking about women who practised witchcraft to keep their men? It would explain Mokdad's behaviour. He hated her even more now that he suspected her of something as terrible as that. He wanted to hurt her, hurt her husband and the elephant she cared for.

He pulled the catapult from his pocket and searched the ground for a stone, then took aim at the animal in the distance. The stone struck Shanti on the back and she made a sound and turned her head round. The woman, who had not seen the stone strike, thought nothing of the animal's reaction and urged her forward with the stick. Calming down, Shanti resumed her languorous pace, head down, her trunk brushing against the grass with a placidity that infuriated Jamil even more. He forgot the woman and turned his attention to the animal. He looked for another stone and waited until Mokdad and the woman had turned their backs to him before shooting again. The stone struck the animal low on the flank, and she jerked away and trumpeted louder than before. This time Olga seemed taken aback. She stroked the animal and tried to calm her down and guide her towards her enclosure, but Shanti refused to move and began to sway from side to side.

The circus workers stopped and watched while the woman spoke to Shanti and tapped her leg with the guide stick, but the elephant did not respond to her gentle commands. Mokdad stood by and Jamil wanted to go up to him and say, 'You see? I did that. I'm not weak. If I can hurt an animal like that so easily I'm just as strong as any man.' They could be friends now because they were equals. He would not hesitate, would not shy away from terrible things, he would never be afraid again. If only Tarek and the other boys who had made fun of him had been there now. His temples throbbed with pride and anger and he looked around for another stone, but could not find any in the hard well-trodden earth of the camp. Frustrated, he remembered the fossil and he took it out of his pocket. He was tempted to use it. The ancient creature lay there in his palm like a good luck charm, a promise that everything would turn out fine. God looked after him. There had to be a God. He could not comprehend a world growing old without purpose.

Standing some distance away, unnoticed by everyone, he loaded the catapult with the fossil and took careful aim at the animal's leg. The shot hit right on the existing wound and Shanti turned and struck Mokdad, who was standing next to her, her trunk catching him on the shoulder with such force that he was thrown to the ground. Immediately she came up to him, lowering her head and slapping her ears against her body. The woman rushed in and struck Shanti with the guide stick, ordering her to move, and the elephant took a couple of steps back before, after a moment of hesitation, charging again, this time at Olga, who hit her with the stick again. But it was not the bullhook; it broke after a few blows and Shanti lowered her head and butted the woman, throwing her up in the air. Olga landed hard on the ground and did not move . The circus hands rushed towards her, shouting and waving their arms. The animal paused and stared at them, while blood from the wound flowed down her leg.

Fifteen

THEY TRIED TO get to Olga and the doctor again and again but Shanti charged them and they scattered, leaving Mokdad and the woman lying on the ground. When the elephant lost interest in that game she vented her anger on the caravans, which she toppled one after another. Then she went to the animal enclosures, tore the steel barriers, flung the pieces about and attacked the zebras, which fled to the fields. While she was doing all that, the circus people tried to carry the man and the woman away, but Shanti turned abruptly and charged again, so they had to drop them and run. The animal returned to the middle of the camp, where she wrapped her trunk around Olga and held her up in the air, the unconscious woman's arms and legs dangling.

That was how Damianos found them when he returned from the town. He asked for the bullhook and slowly approached Shanti, who stood staring at him.

He reached the doctor first and called his men to take him away. This time Shanti did not stop them. He then walked on, ordering the animal to put the woman down, but Shanti held the limp body with her trunk and stood her ground. When he passed the bullhook to his right hand, she could tell that he was going to hurt her and slowly moved backwards. He ordered her again, in a louder voice, but she kept ignoring his command until he had come close to her. Then she put the woman down and with a sudden move charged him. He dodged and dealt her a blow in the ear, which made Shanti cry out and turn away, but the next moment she turned back and attacked him again. He knew that the blow must have hurt and was surprised that it had not been enough to discipline her. When she lowered her head to butt him he swung the bullhook hard and struck her across the face. The blunt hook cut her skin, and this time she retreated several yards and watched him, while blood rolled down her trunk. Once again he waved her towards her enclosure but again she came forward. When he swung the bullhook this time she struck his arm with her trunk and it fell from his hand.

Now that she knew he was unarmed she came towards him without any fear and he knew that she would kill him. But she chased him only for fifty yards or so before returning to the unconscious woman. She lifted her up and put her down close to the circus tent, which she then began to demolish by tearing the canvas with her trunk, kicking the rope anchors out of the ground and knocking down the poles with her head.

Damianos went to his caravan and returned with his Remington and a box of birdshot cartridges, the only ammunition he had. The first shot struck Shanti in the flank and she bolted with a pain much worse than anything she had felt from the bullhook. She stopped some distance away and turned around with her head lowered and ears flattened, bleeding from her flank, lingering at the edge of the camp. The circus owner slung the shotgun over his shoulder and walked quickly towards his wife, but he had just reached her when Shanti charged again. For a few seconds the man stared at the advancing elephant in disbelief, then reached for his gun and fired at her as she was coming at him. The shot struck her in the face and she stopped, trumpeting and shaking her bleeding head.

A few yards away Damianos replaced the spent cartridges and for the first time since his arrival looked around. The boy was there among the people who worked for him, kneeling next to the doctor, and he shouted at him, 'Go away.' Jamil did not move and before turning back to the animal Damianos asked his men to take him away. A small man in a dusty white suit standing among the ruins of his business, he gazed at what remained of it:

the half-collapsed circus tent, the toppled caravans, the demolished enclosures, the zebras scattered in the fields. A calm expression came over his face and he felt a huge relief. He had lost a long time ago. Now at last he had come to terms with his defeat. He worried about Olga, he ought to get help for her, but he could not walk away. Still standing in the distance, the animal made him feel helpless. If only he had long ago admitted to himself how helpless he had always been. It was easy to disguise it. The truth was that until now chance had always decided for him. This was the first time he had been in charge. Whether it was a good or bad decision mattered little, he thought; you could not avoid making bad decisions if you wanted to be in charge of your own life. I was not a good father. I have not grieved for my child. And I have been a bad husband. It does not matter that she has been a bad wife too. It was fine to admit all that now. It was fine to give up hope that anything would ever get better, but he might as well draw a line in the sand. This sort of life was over.

He remained calm when he raised the gun and shot again at the placid animal, pumping and shooting until the shotgun was empty, then, while she turned to get away from him, he reloaded and shot her in the legs. Shanti made a few more steps and fell on her side on the edge of the camp and he walked towards her without hurry, carrying the shotgun and the box with the last few cartridges. He stood very close to her, fed the cartridges into the gun and began to shoot.

But he could not kill her with birdshot. When there were but two cartridges left he loaded them and rested the muzzle behind the top of her front leg, above her heart. Her head lay on the dirt but her eye blinked and stared at him for a moment. Then it turned away, as if he did not matter to her, and it closed. Her brown skin rose up and down under the gun barrel with each breath, she beat her trunk on the dirt a few times and seemed to be falling asleep, as calm and contented as in her afternoon slumbers. He could have sold her and paid off his debts and would have had enough left to leave that place, keep what remained of the business going for another year. It seemed to him that the animal was daring him to kill her, was welcoming her death, taking satisfaction from its prospect as though she knew that she would be ruining him by it. And then she opened her eyes, looked at him again and stretched her trunk feebly in his direction, beckoning him, it seemed, not to delay.

He walked back to where Olga lay. She was coming round—the doctor too—and he wiped her bloodied face with his hand. He felt enough relief to call himself happy as he held her head in his hands.

'Did you just get back?' she asked him. 'Shanti went crazy... Did you tie her up?' It hurt if she tried to move and her arm hung limply in his hand. She said, 'She hurt the doctor. How is he?'

'Don't move, my love,' Damianos said to her. 'I'll get help.'

She raised her head to say something else but her face twisted in pain, and she rested back in his arms. A moment later she tried again. 'I couldn't stop her,' she said, and he nodded and held her. He was calm now that he had nothing to expect, and his only hope was that Olga would get well. Not far away the doctor was being helped to his feet by the circus hands. There was the boy, too, sobbing.

'Where is Shanti?' Olga asked.

He stroked her hair and kept looking at the boy. 'I have something I've been meaning to ask you,' he said. 'I had this idea… Well, perhaps now is not the best time.'

'What is it?' she asked.

'The boy. I've been thinking…'

But he stopped. It was hardly the right time to tell her now, was it? He would have to wait until she was better, and then he would ask her.

Sixteen

THE CAPTAIN stood on the flying bridge, warming his hands with the cup and taking scalding sips as he gazed at the bay trees on the esplanade, the tiled roofs, the bell tower and the grey-brown hills beyond the town. Dry land held very few pleasures for him—in fact he nursed a secret contempt for it. It was too safe over there, life too slow, too predictable whatever anyone said, and so he was not displeased that he was leaving again three days after his arrival, even though he could not claim to have had such a bad time, having spent a few hours with a local woman. He was widowed, lived alone and answered to no one, but he knew that she was married, and so he had agreed to meet her on the ship in the afternoon instead of somewhere in the town; besides, firm floors, unlike the swaying floor of his cabin, unnerved him somehow.

He leant into the speaking tube and told the engineer to start the engines, took another sip of his coffee and stroked his beard. A grinding noise came from far below, a ball of smoke shot up from the funnel, and the steel under his feet began to vibrate. A moment later a cloud of soot, which made him cough, settled on him. He wiped his face with satisfaction. It was not always the case that the engines would start on the first try, and he was happier now, knowing that they would soon be on their way.

In bed that afternoon two days before, as they lay in silence next to each other in his narrow berth and smoked in the dark, she had surprised him with a casual remark: 'The elephant is dead.' The captain had remembered his visit to the circus, nine months earlier, which was when he had first encountered the woman who would become his lover. Since then he had associated the animal with that fortunate meeting and felt a vague fondness and a certain pity for it, too, for having been brought all the way from the jungles of who-knew-where to perform in a cheap provincial circus, kitted out in a pink hat and jingling anklets.

'Did he fall ill?' he had asked.

'He was a she. And it was shot.'

He had learnt the rest of the story from the shipping agent, described in great detail and with a relish that made the captain suspect the man had not been quite faithful to the truth. Nevertheless, the gist of it was that for whatever reason the elephant had run amok, attacked her keeper and wrecked most of the circus camp before her owner killed her with a shotgun. The elephant dead, a large part of the circus equipment ruined and the performers and workers having already gone unpaid for some time, the owner had lost his business to the banks. 'He was already heavily in debt,' the shipping agent had told the captain. 'Two or three months ago he even asked me for a loan, but I had the good sense to refuse. Imagine what would've happened if I'd said yes. I would've lost it all—all!'

When the agent had asked him if he would take the foreign man and the boy to the mainland because the ferry wasn't running again and they had nowhere to stay, he had replied that he did not mind, but the agent should let them know that the ship was very slow and they would be calling at several ports along the way. 'You'll be doing everyone a favour,' the man behind the desk had said. 'There's been nothing but trouble ever since the foreigner with the boy came. He's supposed to be a doctor. And who cares? He hasn't cured anyone here that I know of. The two of them were the first boat people to arrive and they'll be the last to leave. Hopefully, there won't be any more.'

The captain sipped some more of his coffee. The old cargo ship with the rusty hull was the only thing in the world he could call his own—no land, no family, no house. How much more did a man need? He finished his drink and went to his small cabin behind the bridge, where the heating pipes running from the engine room had begun to turn hot. He lay on the berth in his clothes and shoes to catch up on the sleep he had missed the night before. When he returned to the bridge, at around eleven, the helmsman was there. He listened to his subordinate's report while staring out of the window. 'And the passengers are aboard,' the helmsman said. The passengers? Oh, yes, the passengers… Still a little light-headed from sleep, the captain had forgotten about them. In fact he could see them now, the man and the boy—was he his son?—standing shyly on the deck without any luggage while the crew finished loading the cargo. The boy looked dourly in his direction and the captain waved at him from the bridge, but the child did not return his greeting. The captain did not let it affect his jovial mood. When the cargo was aboard he stepped out on to the flying bridge and gave the order to cast off. Back in the steering room, as the ship pushed away from the quay, he gave the whistle a blast just for the hell of it and watched the boy jump at the sudden sound. It made him chuckle.

'We're leaving.' Jamil's voice expanded with excitement, and he leant over the side of the ship to watch the concrete quay slowly move away. 'Look. Do you see?'

Mokdad glanced out at the quay, where a stevedore stared back at him with arms akimbo. He felt the impulse to raise his hand in farewell, but stopped himself. Jamil and he were as much strangers now as they had been when they arrived all those months before.

'When we get to the mainland I'll look for a job,' Jamil said. 'There must be something I could do to make some money. I'll learn the language. You don't have to worry. You'll see. We'll only stay for a few weeks. Until we make enough to last us the rest of the journey.'

If only the sea had taken them to another island, Mokdad thought; there were tens of them in that archipelago.

'I wasn't good at school. I didn't like the teacher,' the boy said. 'She was mean to me. No one liked her. When the war began, she left. One day we went to school and the head teacher came to teach us. We were very happy that she had gone, but the head teacher was even stricter than her. He hit us. When he left, too, I stopped going to school. Will I have to go to school again? In the place we're going to live? I don't need to go, I can learn things on my own, but if I have to…'

He touched Mokdad's sleeve and after a moment held it with unsure fingers, trying to intrude into his contemplation. The ship was out of the port now and he had to raise his voice over the blustery wind to be heard.

'And I want to start going to mosque. It's important, don't you think? God has helped us so much. We could have drowned or…' He didn't want to talk about what had happened with the elephant. 'My mother made me go to mosque. I didn't want to. And the imam made me read and he slapped me if I made a mistake. But I'll go again. I want to be a good Muslim. Couldn't you teach me instead?'

'I don't know much about it,' Mokdad said.

'Don't you go to mosque? Didn't you go to a madrasa when you were my age?'

'Why do you want to learn?'

'Because God only helps those who put their faith in Him,' Jamil said—he had heard it somewhere. He looked at Mokdad and went on, 'We need God's help. We could go to mosque together. Shouldn't we start to pray? I don't know how to. How many times?'

'Five.'

'Yes, yes, five times a day. When is the next one?'

'At noon.'

'And the direction?'

Mokdad pointed towards the east and Jamil looked, as though he expected to see the Kaaba somewhere out in the open sea and the white sky. After a while he sat down beside Mokdad, their shoulders touching, and kicked idly at a coiled hawser. A few minutes into their long voyage and he was bored already. The excitement of having left the island was gone, but he could endure it with the thought that they would be together from now on.

'We need somewhere to sleep,' he said, with an air of responsibility. 'We should ask the captain if there is a cabin we could have. It's a big ship and there are only a few sailors and him. There must be some place.'

'Yes, later.'

'I could cook for us. I used to help my sisters in the kitchen many times, I can do it. You don't have to eat foreign food. Ask the captain to let me cook for you.' He waited for the doctor to say something but Mokdad was quiet. After a moment Jamil asked, 'What did the man say when you gave him back the money?'

'I gave it to his wife.'

'What did she say?' Jamil asked tentatively. 'Was she cross with me? Did she want to call the police?'

'No.'

'What did you tell her?'

'That you were a good boy. That you did it to help me.'

'What did she tell her husband?'

'You must never do that again,' Mokdad said sternly. 'Next time I'll take you to the police myself.'

'No, never. I promise.'

'She was very good to you. It was a mistake not staying with them.'

'And the man won't tell the police?' the boy went on. 'Did he promise you not to?'

Mokdad said quietly, 'They will have forgotten about us by now. They have their own troubles.' His leg had gone numb and he changed position with a grimace of pain. He searched his pockets for the painkillers. He had taken the cast off only the day before.

'Does it hurt?' Jamil said.

'Can you get me some water? Find someone and ask for a glass.'

'Yes.'

Jamil sprang to his feet and went away unsteadily. The sea was rough and the rocking was making him sick. It was another weakness he tried to hide, telling himself that he needed to be strong to help Mokdad, who was still unwell from what had happened. He tried not to think of the incident. A crewman was smoking leaning against the side of the ship and Jamil mimed his request to him. The man pointed him to a door. It was the toilet, but the boy did not try to explain that he did not want to drink himself and went in search of someone else to ask for a glass. His hair was already matted from the wet salty wind. He had left home with shorn hair and now it reached his eyes. Before going inside he looked back at the doctor, who still sat squeezed up against the coiled hawser with his hands in his pockets. How weak he seemed to him now. The desire to look after him swelled up inside him, to nurse him back to health, to make him forget everything that had happened. It would be fine from now on. There would be no more danger, no more people like the circus man and no more women like her. Jamil stared longingly towards him, wondering when he would give way to the temptation to let him know how much he loved him. Not now; it was too soon. And did it matter whether he said it or not? What mattered was that they would be together, always. He went in and climbed the stairway to the bridge. He felt happy.

Mokdad sat alone facing the sea. The cold wind made him shiver but he did not follow Jamil inside. He was relieved to be alone, to not have to answer his questions. Sometimes he disliked the boy with an intensity that made him feel shame. He knew it was unfair. He said to himself, 'I know I am not a good man, I don't need that child to keep reminding me,' and again he was gripped by guilt. All the love that he was capable of, he had always kept for himself. He had never shared it. Olga had seen through him. Perhaps that was the reason why she had rejected him. He looked back but Jamil had gone inside. The pain in his leg was not getting better and he swallowed the pills without water. He remembered how he used to tell his patients, who annoyed him with their complaints, not to be afraid of a little pain.

He caught a glimpse of Jamil in the windows of the wheel room, gesticulating to the captain. Despite his other feelings he still felt a sense of responsibility for him: he could not abandon him. He stood up and attempted to walk off the pain, going in the direction of the stern. The smoking seaman was no longer there. From a fastened open metallic door with steps going down came the noise of the ship's engines. Mokdad hobbled on glumly in the cold morning. Beyond the stern the island was an almost flat grey piece of land, far enough away to not be able to see any houses. It was what he had first seen from the upturned dinghy, too. He found somewhere to sit and rest his leg. Staring at the distant island, he counted the weeks, then the days that Jamil and he had spent there, and it seemed to him that if it were not for his injured leg he could convince himself that most of the things he remembered had not actually happened: the circus had not existed, he had never met Olga, and the tailor had drowned by himself.

But the pain in his leg, dulled by the pills now, would not let him deceive himself. He remembered Jamil being at his bedside when he was recovering, saying nothing, just staring at him. He had been there even at night. Once

Mokdad had woken up to find him asleep, the boy's swagger gone, the sullenness on his face swept away by the calmness of sleep, just a little child curled up in an armchair pushed against the bed.

The first blast of the whistle startled him. There was a second, then a third. He did not understand why. He felt the ship changing direction and he went to see what was happening. Leaning against the side, he searched the rough sea with his eyes but could not see anything. Then he caught sight of something, which quickly disappeared behind the waves. He stood there a moment, gazing out into the distance, until he saw it again: a large inflatable boat, a bit like the one the boy and he had travelled in but much bigger, full of people. He could see their heads bobbing above the side of their boat while the waves tossed it about. As the ship came closer it became clear that the boat was adrift and the people were waving for help. He could not hear them. They were still far away and the wind was blowing in their direction. He watched, his hair streaming, the wind spraying him with seawater. The ship's whistle sounded three blasts again and the crew members prepared to launch a lifeboat.

When the ship was close enough to see faces it stopped; the lifeboat was lowered and powered towards the drifting refugees. It went back and forth, carrying them to the ship. Men, women and children with pieces of luggage stood shivering with cold on the deck, thanking the captain. Mokdad did not approach them. He watched them from where he stood at the stern, listening to them cheer in his mother tongue. Jamil came and stood with him, saying nothing, too. Then the captain came. He said in English, 'We have to turn back. There are more than fifty. We can't take care of them. Not enough food or water. The next port of call is a full day away. We'll be back on the island in a couple of hours.'

'What is he saying?' Jamil asked.

'We are going back,' Mokdad said, and then, to reassure the boy, he added, 'It'll be only for a few hours.'

'Do you speak their language?' the captain asked him. 'Yes.'

'I hear you're a doctor.'

'Yes.'

'Good. Come on then, let's see if they need any help. Translate for me. Your son can help the little ones.'

'Who?' Mokdad said without thinking. 'No, no. He...'

'The boy. Isn't he your son, man?'

Mokdad opened his mouth to deny it, to tell the truth, to clear up the misunderstanding once and for all. Then he hesitated. In that moment he saw, blurred as if through frosted glass, himself at home before the war, on his journey, in the dinghy, face to face with the man he would later kill, and with the boy at sea. And he saw again the circus and the woman during their long walks and the dead elephant lying on the muddy camp ground—all that passed through his mind before he replied.

Sign up to our mailing list at
www.myriadeditions.com
Follow us on Facebook and Twitter

About the author

PANOS KARNEZIS was born in Greece and came to the UK in 1992, where he worked in industry before starting to write. He is the author of four novels—*The Maze* (shortlisted for the Whitbread First Novel Award), *The Birthday Party*, *The Convent* and *The Fugitives*, and a collection of stories, *Little Infamies*. His work is translated into several languages.